# ALL'S FAIR IN LOVE AND SCANDAL

## By Caroline Linden

# ALL'S FAIR
# IN LOVE AND
# SCANDAL

## CAROLINE LINDEN

AVONIMPULSE
*An Imprint of HarperCollinsPublishers*

EPub Edition APRIL 2015 ISBN: 9780062419071

Print Edition ISBN: 9780062419088

10 9 8 7 6

# ALL'S FAIR IN LOVE AND SCANDAL

# CHAPTER ONE

**D**ouglas Bennet, handsome, charming and heir to a baronet, had reached the age of twenty-nine with very little in the way of adversity or disappointment.

His life had been blessed from the start. He was the only son of Sir George Bennet, baronet. It wasn't an illustrious title, but it was an ancient one and it came with a large fortune. His mother was the daughter of a former war secretary, and his uncle was the Earl of Doncaster, who had the King's ear. It was the best possible combination of circumstances, with impressive connections yet no onerous personal responsibility.

He was tall, with a muscular build and an abundance of good health. He was also excessively fond of sport, and was most at home in the boxing ring, with a fencing foil in his hand, or atop a fast horse. Not even a taste for spirits kept him from being trim and strong to a degree other men envied. In addition, he was a handsome fellow, with thick auburn hair and hazel eyes, and possessed a good-humored charm that made him popular with other men and a great favorite among the ladies.

Even his main fault sprang from all these advantages. With his life comfortable and privileged in nearly every regard, Douglas was bent on adventure and excitement. As a boy he was constantly getting into trouble, immune to his mother's lectures on proper behavior or any punishment she imposed. As a youth he became known for his pranks; nothing was too daring or outrageous for him to attempt. By the time he was a young man, it was wagering, on anything that offered a good contest. After one significant loss, his father had taken him on a tour of the Fleet Prison, where debtors went, and told him frankly that the Fleet was his future if he didn't show some restraint. After that Douglas took care, but only to the point of never wagering more than he could afford to lose. Thanks to his generous allowance, to say nothing of good luck, this had only a slight impact on his activities.

For nearly eighteen years his most frequent companion in all this hell-raising good fun had been Tristan Burke. They'd met as boys at school and recognized each other as kindred spirits at once. Burke was, quite simply, the best mate an adventurous boy could want. He was bold, daring, unfettered by propriety, willing to wager on anything, and had a wicked sense of humor and fun that only improved with age.

At times Douglas envied him fiercely. His friend's parents had died when he was a child, and Burke had come into his enormous inheritance at the age of twenty-one, with no limits or oversight. Douglas didn't envy Burke's lack of family, much—only when his mother started prodding him to marry, or his sister barged into his house and rousted him from bed at an ungodly hour of the morning—but he rather fancied the idea of being completely free. However much he might deny it, Douglas knew in his heart he'd have to settle down one day. It would kill his mother and deeply disappoint his father if he didn't, and Douglas was too fond of his parents to do that. Still, he planned to put it off for as long as possible, and certainly as long as Burke did.

It was nothing less than a thunderous shock when Tristan Burke abruptly got married—to Douglas's sister Joan, of all people. Douglas had been away from town when he got the news, and at first he didn't believe it. Not that Joan would marry; he knew she wanted to be married, and that his mother had begun to despair of finding her a husband. Joan was tall for a girl and she could be very impertinent, especially when she decided to tease him. But Burke had called Joan a Fury mere weeks before he stood up beside her in the church and pledged himself to her for better or for worse. Despite Douglas's suspicions that something scandalous must have forced Burke into it, he couldn't determine what. His parents refused to speak of it, and Burke just grinned. In fact, Burke looked pleased. And instead of spending his nights tearing through London, he stayed at home with Joan.

Douglas had other friends, but none of them had Burke's audacity, his humor, his energy. He couldn't say he was sorry to have Burke for a brother-in-law, but he was very sorry to have lost such a jovial companion. Not having Burke around, ready with a sly comment or wager, took some of the verve out of his usual rakish activities.

"Well, well, back to your usual haunts," drawled William Spence one evening as Douglas strolled through a ballroom in search of amusement but finding himself at loose ends.

"I was away from town." He propped one shoulder against the wall. "It's dashed quiet tonight." It was. The card room was filled with old women and timid men playing for shilling stakes. Aside from Spence, he didn't see any of his normal companions. First Burke, now everyone else of spirit had abandoned him. Perhaps he should just go to a gaming hell for the rest of the evening.

"Ghastly dull," concurred Spence languidly. "I don't know why I come to these parties."

"There's always the wine." He lifted a glass from a passing footman's tray and raised it in salute.

Spence clicked his tongue. "So tame! Not like the courageous man of adventure I once knew."

He laughed. That was Spence's way of goading someone into a prank or wager. "Adventure! In Lady Creighton's ballroom?"

"Just because it's quiet tonight doesn't mean there's no sport to be had." Spence tilted his head and nodded toward a distant corner of the room. "There, for instance. A lovely woman, standing and watching others, far less beautiful than she, dance and be merry."

Douglas looked at the woman in question and felt a flicker of surprise. For once Spence was right. She was a beauty, no question, and yet she seemed isolated and alone. "Who is she?"

"Madeline Wilde." Spence watched him expectantly, but Douglas had never heard of her and only shrugged. A thin smile spread over the other man's face. "An unusual woman. A widow, of course. She comes to all the best society events but never dances. No one quite knows if she's made of ice, or merely too good for mortal men."

By now he was all but staring at her. Her hair shone like gold under the chandeliers, and her bosom looked plump and perfect in the deep green bodice of her low-cut gown. "Never dances? Why?"

"No one can fathom. It's become something of a challenge in certain quarters to see what will entice her. More than one fellow's lost a few guineas over her."

His pulse jumped. Dance with such a woman *and* win a contest? He was helpless to resist. "I wager I could persuade her," he murmured, his eyes tracing the slope of her bared shoulder.

"Five pounds says you shan't," said Spence at once.

"Done." Douglas tugged his jacket straight and winked at his friend. "I'll expect it in coin tomorrow." And he sauntered off through the crowd, looking forward to making her acquaintance.

## CHAPTER TWO

"Quite a crush, isn't it?" He gave Mrs. Wilde his winning smile, the easy, friendly one that soothed anxious nerves and made women of every age and rank like him.

She turned at his voice behind her. Something like mirth glimmered in her eyes. "Indeed."

"I hardly know a soul here tonight." He lowered his voice but without leaning toward her. Leaning put women on guard. A low voice made them lean toward *him*, which he much preferred. "It's rather intimidating, to tell the truth."

"You?" She arched one golden brow. "You don't seem the sort to be easily intimidated."

Douglas grinned. He knew he was a big fellow. Women tended to like it once they got to know him. "Rubbish. I'm petrified just looking at the elegance of this assembly."

Her lovely lips curved. Her head tipped toward him, just a little. Her dark eyes gleamed. "I don't believe you."

"It's true," he protested. "My heart is racing, my knees are unsteady. Look—see how my hand trembles." He caught her hand in his, tensing his muscle to produce the tiniest tremor in his hand, and then relaxing it. "Ah. Your touch has healing power, I see."

She left her hand in his, but that slight smile tugging at her mouth grew a bit wider. "It's not flattering to a woman, to say her touch calms a man's heart and body. Usually she wishes it were the other way around."

His heart did skip a beat at that. She was a flirt; excellent. He adored flirts. Douglas stroked his thumb over the back of her hand. "It only stilled the terror, my dear. I suspect you could elicit an entirely different sort of tremor." He lifted her hand and brushed the faintest kiss over her knuckles. "We must be introduced."

"I fear there's no one here in this quiet corner who will do it." Her eyes seemed to grow darker as he drew one finger across her palm.

"Then I will risk being appallingly rude and present myself." He bowed over her hand, his eyes never leaving her face. "Douglas Bennet, at your service."

"Yes, I know."

"You do?" He smiled in delight. "Then we should become acquainted . . ."

"Mr. Douglas Bennet," she repeated, her voice changing just enough to freeze him in place. "Son and heir of Sir George Bennet, baronet. A very handsome title, an even handsomer fortune. An unrepentant rake, gambler, brawler, and sometime rogue. Your mother wants you to marry; you couldn't be less interested. Your taste runs to tavern maids and opera dancers, preferably French. Your sister wed your bosom friend Lord Burke, much to your disgust, although no one quite knows if you pity your sister or your onetime friend more." She tilted her head and smiled as he stared at her, blank-faced with shock that was rapidly turning to indignation. "What have I forgotten? Oh yes—you love a good wager. What was the one that sent you over here: a wager to get me into your bed?" She slipped her fingers from his slackened grip. "If it was . . . you've already lost. I hope you didn't stake a large amount."

"It was merely for the pleasure of a dance," he said, hiding his temper behind a flat tone.

She laughed. By God, she had a beautiful laugh, throaty and soft, the sort that made a man want to amuse her so he could hear it again. "I doubt it. But then, you're also accustomed to losing, aren't you?" She sank into a graceful curtsy, giving him one last view of her matchless bosom. "Good evening, sir." She turned and walked away, unhurried, unaffected.

He was still standing there, pulsing with unexpected desire and insulted pride, when Spence slung an arm around his neck. "Rough luck," he said, his voice brimming with amusement. "She's a cold one." He grinned and slapped Douglas's shoulder. "Five quid, gone in a blink."

Douglas turned a black look on the man. "You didn't say when."

Spence raised his eyebrows, still grinning like a cardsharp. Come to think of it, he usually looked like that, right before he took someone's money. Douglas had won and lost to Spence with equanimity—for the most part—but tonight he wanted to punch his friend. Spence had deliberately dared him to an impossible task, sending him over to be humiliated and rejected. And now he wanted five pounds. "What do you mean?"

"You didn't say *when.*" Douglas bit off each word. "She rejected me tonight, but there's always tomorrow night, and the next, and the next after that."

A scowl darkened Spence's face for a split second before he threw up his hand. "You're right! I didn't. Let's say . . . within a fortnight. That ought to be enough time to work up some charm and get between the fair widow's legs."

"You wagered for a dance, not a tupping."

"Well." Spence's eyes glittered. "I thought I wagered for tonight. Allowances must be made." When Douglas said nothing, Spence leaned closer. "You're not afraid, are you? Not going soft in the head like Burke? The woman gutted you and denied you in front of all society, man. Look around." He swept one arm toward the rest of the room. "Don't you think half the people here guessed why you sought her out? And now they see her leaving alone, and you looking like she took your ballocks with her."

Against his will, Douglas's eyes caught on Madeline Wilde as she made her way toward the doors. Damn, she was beautiful. He *had* wanted to dance with her, and probably get her into bed as well, even though she was not, as she had so baldly pointed out, his usual type of woman. She was . . . something more.

As if she could hear his thoughts, she paused at the top of the short flight of stairs leading out of the ballroom. She glanced back over her shoulder, and her eyes met his. For a moment he felt again a bolt of lust—unwanted this time—

and her lips curved, as if she knew. She lowered her chin and smiled in a coy, entrancing way, as if they shared secrets—or as if she dared him to uncover hers. With breathtaking nerve, she pursed up her lips as if in a kiss, and touched one finger to them.

He took a harsh breath as she turned and continued on her way, her emerald skirts swaying bewitchingly. "Why her?"

"Why not her?"

Douglas set his jaw. "You had her marked before I stepped into this room. I saw you watching her, Spence. A former lover? Was I supposed to exact some revenge or retribution by asking the lady to dance?"

"The courtesan's daughter?" The other man's lip curled. "Hardly a former lover of mine. I have higher standards than that."

Not really, in Douglas's opinion. Spence liked married women who couldn't impose on his freedom, and who often wished to keep their liaisons secret. That was hardly what one could call a refined requirement. Still, Douglas hadn't known she was a courtesan's daughter. He made a mental note to find out more about that.

"She appeared respectable enough to me," he said.

"To *you*," repeated Spence with an edge of condescension. "Compared to a tavern wench with rounded heels, she might be. To the rest of us . . ." He snapped his fingers at a passing footman and took a glass of wine from the man's tray. "You really ought to improve your taste, Bennet."

Douglas let that go. He did like tavern wenches. They were friendly and earthy, nothing delicate or prim about them. They were more willing to be adventurous in bed, and they demanded so much less of him—financially and emotionally—than any other woman would.

"But why her?" he asked again, circling back to his main question. "Just for the sport of it? Or did you simply want the pleasure of seeing me turned down flat?"

Spence didn't reply for a moment. His eyes were sharp and calculating. "How plump are your pockets at the moment?" he finally asked.

"Reasonably," said Douglas. He'd been gone from town for a month overseeing repairs at one of his father's estates, to the great benefit of his purse. Still, it was a few weeks to quarter day, when his father paid out his allowance. He could always find a use for more money.

Spence lowered his voice. "I suspect our lovely Mrs. Wilde of being more than she appears. And if I'm right, there's two thousand quid to be had."

Douglas's eyebrows shot up. "What is she, a spy?"

"Of some sort," muttered Spence. "You aren't acquainted with a little piece of rubbish called *50 Ways to Sin*, are you?"

"No."

"Get a copy. It's a pamphlet of a most . . . intriguing nature." A cunning smile split his face. "I suspect you'll enjoy it."

That smile put him on guard. Douglas might not be the most discerning fellow, but he wasn't stupid, and he knew Spence too well. "If you insist—not that it answers my question about why you wanted me to charm my way into Mrs. Wilde's good graces."

"The authoress is unknown. I daresay you'll guess why when you read it. But she's piqued more than one man's pride with her scandalous pen, and there's a bounty out

for her name. Mrs. Wilde seems a very likely candidate."
He shrugged. "If you can unmask her, I'll split the bounty
with you."

Douglas folded his arms and looked at Spence through
narrowed eyes. "I should seduce the woman, gain her con-
fidence, presumably enough to be admitted to her boudoir,
where I would have to search for some proof that she writes
this pamphlet. And for that, you'll take half the money? Not
so, Spence, not so."

His friend's hooded eyes flashed. "Very well. Forget I said
anything."

Douglas shrugged. "Hard to do that. Who staked the
bounty?"

Spence hesitated.

"If the bloke's serious about finding the author, he can't be
too secretive about it."

"Lord Chesterton," said Spence with obvious reluctance.
"He felt she identified him too clearly in one story and he's
livid."

"Identified? She didn't use his name?"

Spence looked impatient. "No, she uses obviously false
names."

"Then how did he recognize himself?"

His friend smirked again. "Find a copy and see if you can
deduce that yourself."

Douglas wondered what on earth this story was that
would drive Lord Chesterton to such an action. The man
was as correct and polite as anyone could be, distantly connected to the King and as stiff as a piece of kindling. Now
he'd placed a public bounty on a woman's head? What could

Mrs. Wilde—if she was in fact the author—have written about him? Two thousand pounds was a small fortune, and certain to attract a fair amount of attention.

Of course, that also made it a much more interesting contest.

"Three to one," he said after a moment's thought.

"Eh?"

"Three to one split, if we take the bounty." He glanced at Spence. "You're the one, obviously."

"Two to three," countered the other man.

"Do it yourself, then."

Spence muttered a few curses under his breath, but stuck out his hand. "Done."

Douglas shook on it, already anticipating his next meeting with the wily widow. "Done."

## CHAPTER THREE

**M**adeline Wilde was almost relieved when Douglas Bennet gave her an excuse to leave the crowded and rather dull ball. Her deliciously fashionable shoes were beginning to pinch, and she was tired. When she had claimed her cloak, she stepped out onto the broad steps of Creighton House and took a deep breath of cool night air. Even ripe with the scent of horses, it was refreshing.

Given the size of the ball, there were a number of carriages for hire loitering nearby. It was only a short journey to her house, but she wasn't about to walk. Just closing the carriage door between her and the dark night outside made her breathe easier, and within ten minutes the hired hack stopped in front of her house. "One shilling, ma'am," said the driver.

She stepped down and handed him the money. "Plus an extra, sir, if you remain here until I'm safely inside." She showed him the promised shilling.

"Expecting trouble?"

"No," she said, "but a lady alone at night cannot be too cautious. Will you wait?"

He hesitated, then put out his hand. "Aye."

She gave him her best, most grateful, smile as she handed over the coin. She'd learned to choose her drivers carefully after one took her extra shilling and drove off early. But this man had a kind face and she sensed he'd keep his word. "Thank you."

The key was already in her other hand. She walked briskly to her door and put it in the lock. Her maid would come to the door if she knocked, but Madeline didn't want to wait on the step. She couldn't quite put her finger on anything threatening, but lately she'd been dogged by a suspicion that someone was following her. She lived on a moderately quiet square, yet for the last fortnight, there always seemed to be a man lingering nearby when she arrived home. No matter how often she told herself she was being silly—there were drunks everywhere, and it was a public street, where anyone might walk at any hour of the day or night—she couldn't shake a slight feeling of unease. Now she carried her own key and did her best to make certain someone was about, even just a hack driver.

For a moment Douglas Bennet's face—and figure— flashed through her mind. No one would bother her if she had a man like that at her side. And he certainly could make her heart race, for reasons both good and bad. She wondered what had brought him over to the quiet corner where she lurked tonight. Mr. Bennet was notorious for his wagering, but when he leaned over her and focused that heart-stopping smile on her . . .

Mercifully the lock turned. It had grown a bit tempera-mental of late and didn't always open at once. With a sigh of relief, she slipped into her house. From the street, the hack driver touched his cap and said a quiet "G' night, ma'am." She raised one hand in thanks and shot the bolt as the hack drove off, its wheels rattling loudly in the midnight quiet.

Madeline felt the peace of the house envelop her. The quiet was very welcome after the din of the ball, and she took a deep breath, glad to be home. Carefully she lifted her hood free of her hair and took off her gloves. Like her cloak, they were warm, thick green velvet lined with silk, and one of Arthur's last gifts to her before he died. She'd taken good care of both, for it made her feel a little bit of him was still here, comforting her.

"Home at last." Constance, her maid, hurried down the stairs. "I just stepped away for a moment, madam."

"There's no need to apologize." Madeline untied the cloak and shrugged it off. "I'm considering hiring a regular driver, to avoid taking hacks all the time."

"An excellent thought!" The maid took the cloak. "Hire a strapping one who will sleep in the kitchen."

Madeline raised one brow. "I must not give you enough work to do."

"Just observing that if you're going to have a man about the house, he ought to be a fine, big one able to defend us."

"And handsome to look at." Madeline tried not to think of Mr. Bennet again.

"Wouldn't hurt a bit," agreed Constance without a blush. "Someone tall and dark-haired, with piercing blue eyes. He'd be called Jeremy, or Philip, or some other posh name . . ."

"We shall have to make do without him for at least one

more night." She rubbed her bare arms, feeling the chill. "I'll take some tea in my room."

"Yes, madam." Constance hurried off toward the kitchen. She was a very efficient and capable maid, despite her sauciness.

Madeline climbed the stairs to her private sitting room and bedroom. The rooms were meant to be used as adjoining bedrooms, but since she had no husband now, the second room was her personal retreat. The whole house was hers, but somehow this small room was special. Here she felt completely at ease, able to do as she pleased and say what she thought—and most importantly, write what earned her keep.

Constance had left the fire banked, and she stopped to stir it up. It was cool tonight, and without the crush of guests in a ballroom, her fashionable gown was inadequate. For a moment she stood in front of the fireplace, soaking in the warmth from the reviving fire. Unbidden, the thought ran across her mind that she could have had Mr. Bennet here tonight, and he would have kept her warm all night long.

*Warm until morning, when he would leave without a word,* she told herself. She had more important things to think about than that man, even if he really was a handsome devil. "Mr. Nash! Where are you?" When there was no stirring in the room, she lit a lamp, holding it high. "Mr. Nash," she scolded. "Come sit by the fire with me."

With a wide yawn, Mr. Nash emerged from his hiding place, a knitted throw on the chaise longue by the window.

Stretching his legs, he strolled forward as if he hadn't a care in the world.

"You heartless creature," she told him. "It was too much to hope you'd keep my chair warm, wasn't it?"

For answer he only yawned again. Madeline bent down and picked up the black and white cat, scratching under his chin until a loud purr rumbled through his body. She smiled. "I know what you want. You're so predictable, Mr. Nash." He kneaded his paws against her shoulder. She kept scratching his neck until a careless claw snagged on her gown, at which point she reluctantly put him down. He'd ruined a bodice last week and she was particularly fond of this one.

"Just like a male, to tear at a lady's clothing with no thought for her convenience." Mr. Nash seemed to shrug it off. He began licking his paw and swiping it over his ear, almost like a dandy primping for a night out. It brought a smile to her face, imagining him strutting among the female cats of London.

She took off her bracelets and swung a shawl around her shoulders. From a small box on the mantel she produced a key, which unlocked her writing desk near the fireplace. Madeline set out her materials, mentally framing her narrative. Sometimes she wished for more company than Mr. Nash, who was an excellent listener but a terrible conversationalist. He also had a tendency to lie down on top of her papers and smudge her ink, which had led to him being banned from the desk. When she pulled her chair out, Mr. Nash leapt lightly into her lap and curled up, hiding his face under one paw. She gave his ears one last scratch, then opened her ink and took up her pen.

But instead of writing her usual piece, breathless with suggestion and slyly underpinned with innuendo, she found herself hesitating. Again the infuriating Mr. Bennet swaggered across her mind's eye, unspeakably fit and impossibly charming. If she hadn't known who he was, Madeline was half afraid she would have fallen for him tonight. Observing him from across ballrooms hadn't prepared her for the sheer size of him, or the force of his charm, or the warmth behind his smile. In her experience, rakes were predators, serpents in disguise, and if one observed closely, there was a coldness at the core of them. Mr. Bennet, though, seemed to hum with energy and life and blazing hot interest—and all of it focused on her.

Well. She prepared her pen, forcing her mind away from him. He wasn't the first man to look at her that way, and he probably wouldn't be the last. After all, she did encourage it in certain situations. It made her job much easier, and she was hardly immune to a little flattery. What woman didn't enjoy being the subject of a handsome man's attention? The fact that she knew it was only transient made it easier to refuse them, but in their first rush of determination and desire, some gentlemen were quite charming and amusing.

It was less enjoyable now that they'd started wagering about her, though. She thought about that, trying to consider all the possibilities. Mr. Bennet had admitted that he approached her on a wager, although a fairly stupid one in her opinion. A dance? That was all he wanted? She would have sworn not . . .

"Here we are, madam." Constance's entrance with the tea jerked her out of her thoughts. "I brought the brandy as well, since it's cool out."

"Thank you." She took the tea her maid poured and sipped it with a sigh of contentment.

"Do you think you'll be late tonight?" Constance picked up the discarded bracelets and put them away.

If she could keep her thoughts away from charming rogues, it shouldn't take long to write her piece. "No, I don't think so."

"Do you need anything else, then?"

Madeline shook her head. She could dress for bed without help. "There's no need for you to stay up. Go to bed, Constance."

The girl gave her a grateful grin. "Sleep well, madam." She let herself out and closed the door.

Madeline finished her first cup of tea and poured a second. The tea banished the chill from her fingers, and the respite steadied her thoughts. Douglas Bennet was a rogue like many others. Just because she found him more physically appealing didn't mean he was different from the rest. He would have to be another one of her mystery men, alluded to in her work. It made her smile. Perhaps there was a benefit to her unexpected fascination with him after all. She picked up her pen and set to work.

The clock struck three before she finished, poking her pen back into the ink pot and stretching her cramped fingers. She scratched Mr. Nash's head as she read over what she'd written. Yes, it would serve.

"Let's go to sleep," she told her cat, who barely woke enough to meow at her for carrying him into the bedroom and depositing him on the bed. "That's enough for one night."

She thought no more about it until the afternoon, when she went to her weekly appointment at Wharton's Bank. Mr. Sloan, the manager, showed her into the back office as usual. But this time, unusually, the man she'd come to meet was already there, standing in front of the desk with his arms crossed over his chest.

"Liam." She gave him her hand. "Punctual, for a change."

Liam MacGregor smiled. "Perhaps I've decided to mend my ways."

Madeline regarded him as she seated herself. "What is it really? Often I wait half an hour for you." She opened her reticule and took out the papers she'd written last night. "Here you are."

He took them and hesitated a moment, tapping the packet against the desk beside him. "Will I find aught of Douglas Bennet in here?"

She didn't reply, struck motionless by the name. How on earth . . . ?

"I ask," he went on, slowly and carefully, "because it's not yet four o'clock, and already I've heard you made a fool of him last night."

"A fool!" She laughed in surprise. "He asked me to dance. I refused. He asked again, and I left him. If this makes a man a fool—"

"Whatever you said, it left him standing there looking furious, and then—in the words of one old biddy—you laughed in his face and pranced away."

Madeline's mouth flattened. "I do not prance."

Liam gave a sharp bark of laughter and prowled around the small office as though he longed to smash something. "You've never seen yourself walk away, my dear. To a man deep in lust, there might be an element of prancing to your walk."

She shot to her feet. "Is there? Here, tell me if you notice it as I walk away from you right now."

He waved one hand irritably. "Sit down. I'm not dying of lust for you."

"Thank heavens," she murmured, reluctantly sinking back into her chair.

"God save me if ever I made that mistake," he agreed. "I thought you knew how to turn them down sweetly."

"I do." She did. And yet . . . she hadn't really made the effort with Mr. Bennet. She had been blunt and almost crude to his face. Not that it mattered. "Are you frightened because someone is whispering that I teased him? You must know it helps me do my job to tease a man now and then. Besides, he asked for it. He approached me. My every lighthearted word, he batted aside. He was persistent, and he grew distracting. Yes, I sent him away, and if he wasn't amused by the manner of it, I plead guilty." She shrugged. "I wasn't amused by his attentions."

Liam gave her a narrow-eyed stare. "If you're certain," he said at last, grudgingly. "I was surprised to hear of it, that's all."

Not half as surprised as Madeline was to hear that her

encounter with Mr. Bennet was being talked about, so soon and so widely. Besides Madeline herself, Liam had one source of information: his mother. Mrs. MacGregor was very fond of gossip, but she wasn't part of the same social circles as Madeline, let alone Douglas Bennet. Mrs. MacGregor hadn't been at the ball last night, and quite likely none of her friends had been, either. If she'd already heard of it, all of London must be murmuring about it. "If you didn't take tea with your mother every day, you wouldn't have heard anything to trouble you."

He grinned. "I know. But it makes her happy and gives me a chance to gather real intelligence."

"As if the sales numbers are not enough to persuade you that I gather real intelligence," she said wryly. "Are you concerned about something else? It isn't like you to take gossip so seriously—not in this way," she amended quickly.

"Gossip is my business." He tucked her latest effort into his coat pocket. "But from time to time, I worry about you."

Madeline felt a little touched in spite of herself. She knew he meant it in a brotherly way. Liam could be impatient and cutting with her at times, but she never doubted he would rush to her aid if she asked him. "That's not part of our partnership."

"No, but Arthur was one of my dearest friends. I'd sooner spit on his grave than allow you to get into trouble with a hotheaded scoundrel, especially when you were working on our little venture. If Bennet bothers you, tell me."

Her gaze strayed to the corner of paper she could see peeking from his pocket. Perhaps she should take it back and edit a few details . . . Liam almost surely would, when he read what she'd written. She shook off her doubts. If Mr.

Bennet spared another thought for her, it would be one of annoyance or disdain. "I doubt he will. He doesn't have the single-minded determination to cause me trouble. Tonight or tomorrow a new woman will catch his fancy, and the old biddies will find something, and someone, else to talk of." She crossed the room and brushed a light kiss on his cheek. "But you're very kind to worry about me, Liam."

"Be careful," he warned her. "No amount of money is worth you getting hurt in any way."

Madeline said nothing. She didn't want to get hurt, either, but she wasn't afraid of Douglas Bennet. Her work with Liam probably put her in much greater danger.

"Is it good?" Liam tapped his pocket where her writing rested, visibly shrugging off the unpleasant subject.

"As good as ever, I suppose." She was just as happy to let it drop.

"Then it's brilliant." He grinned again. "I must admit, you've been absolutely right about this partnership. I thought it was daft, but I was wrong."

"At least you came to your senses. Arthur would have been gravely disappointed if you hadn't." Her late husband had left her very little money, but numerous partnerships and investments. Some of them had been worth a little, some worth nothing, but her share of Liam's struggling printing business had proved worth more than all the rest combined, especially once Liam agreed to try her ideas and let her be a true partner. She had one invaluable asset—her position in society, with access to all its gossip and scandal—and he was ever in want of something titillating to print for that same society's entertainment. Putting them together had been the perfect match.

"I doubt he would have expected this, but he'd be pleased just the same," said Liam dryly. "Still, try not to *cause* the gossip, will you?"

"For you," she said with a smile.

It was an easy promise to make. She'd wager Douglas Bennet would forget all about her. And she . . . she would try to do the same for him.

## Chapter Four

In the clear light of day, Douglas realized his error.

He had fallen into a bit of a trap. Any wager Spence proposed usually had some hidden facet that favored his own position. If Douglas had remembered that instead of being dazzled by the lady's face, he could have spared himself some humiliation.

However, a wager, once placed, could not be abandoned. The less likely he was to win it, the more determined Douglas was to go down fighting. As of now, he knew almost nothing about Madeline Wilde or the pamphlet Spence claimed she wrote. Two thousand pounds—or the fifteen hundred that would be his share of the winnings—was a considerable prize, but aside from that, he was curious about the beautiful Mrs. Wilde. Fortunately he knew exactly who could tell him more, and now that she was married, he wouldn't even have to feel guilty about asking her. He went to Hanover Square and rang the bell of a house with scaffolding still covering the front of it.

"How goes it, sister?" he greeted the mistress of the house when he was shown into the drawing room.

"Very well, thank you." Joan, Lady Burke, eyed him curiously. She must be shocked to see him calling on her. "And you?"

"Well enough."

"What brings you here?"

He thought of all the things he could say to torment her. He could tell her he'd heard a particularly intriguing rumor, and then refuse to say what it was. He could put on an act of indignation that she'd married his best mate and left him to the mercies of blokes like Spence. At least Tristan Burke had never set him up to look like a fool—not deliberately, at any rate. Douglas certainly felt like one when he received his father's terse note, summoning him posthaste back to London for Burke's wedding to Joan.

He decided on a direct frontal assault. Joan talked too much when she was flustered, and he wanted to know everything. "Have you ever heard of *50 Ways to Sin*?"

His sister froze, her eyes wide. "What?"

"*Fifty Ways to Sin*," he repeated.

"No!"

Slowly Douglas grinned. She'd said it too quickly and too loudly. And as he watched her, Joan blushed bright pink. She did that when she lied.

"I have absolutely no idea what you're talking about." She snatched up her teacup and took a long sip.

"Oh really? Come, Joan," he wheedled. "I'll find out anyway. You might as well tell me."

"If you'll find out anyway, there's no need for you to badger me about it."

"You should be flattered! I've come to you first, trusting in your intelligence and discretion."

Her eyes narrowed. Douglas kept his grin in place but inwardly he cursed; he'd gone too far. "You've never said anything half so nice to me," she accused. "Why do you want to know about that silly story so badly?"

"What kind of story is it?"

She blushed again. "They're rubbish. Not that I read them."

"More than one story, then."

Joan shot him a filthy glare. "Go away, Douglas. I need to supervise the packing. Tristan wants to visit Wildwood and we're leaving in a few days."

"As you wish," he said easily. "Is he in?"

His sister had started to rise, but sat back down at his question. "Why?"

He raised one shoulder. "Perhaps he knows what it is. Burke will tell me, as one gentleman to another."

She seemed to do some rapid thinking. "No, he won't."

"Why wouldn't he?" Douglas grinned again. "These stories grow more and more intriguing."

Joan recovered herself. She smiled back at him. "Buy one and see for yourself."

"Perhaps I will."

Her smirk grew. "Do that."

He cleared his throat, realizing he'd boxed himself into a corner. "Where might I obtain one?"

She burst into laughter. "How did you hear about them, yet learn absolutely nothing about them?"

"I heard it mentioned in passing."

"Oh? By whom?" Now she was interested. Joan loved a good gossip. That was why he'd come to her, after all.

Douglas hesitated. A man's wagers were private, and this one could hardly be discussed with a lady, let alone one's sister. "Some bloke at a ball."

"A man?" Joan blinked. "What did he say?"

Curse Spence; he hadn't said anything at all. "He said I might find it interesting. Given the title, he might be right." Douglas wiggled his eyebrows. "Please tell me they are tales of debauchery and every sort of wickedness."

Instead of snorting with laughter as expected, his sister blushed again. "Run out of ideas for your evening entertainments, have you?"

He stared. "They are? You're not teasing me, are you, Joan?" This wager might have become doubly fascinating.

"I haven't said a word!" But her face was ruby red.

Before Douglas could assure her that she'd revealed a great deal, if not in words, his brother-in-law chose that moment to appear. Tristan, Lord Burke, stopped in the doorway with his usual cocky expression. "Bennet! How odd to see you in daylight."

"He was just going," said Joan in a rush. "Weren't you, Douglas? I think Mother might be planning to stop in for tea today . . ."

"A pleasure to see you, Burke," said Douglas, ignoring his sister. "I thought it was time to see if my sister's driven you mad yet."

Burke's eyes slid to Joan, who blushed again. He sat down beside his wife, draping his arms over the back of the settee. "What do you really want?"

"I came for tea," he protested. Burke just gave him a look indicating he didn't believe that for one moment. Douglas bit back a curse; Burke knew him too well. "And for gossip." He flashed a winning smile. "Naturally I thought of my dear sister, who has a fondness for such things. I was asking her if she knew about a story called *50 Ways to Sin*."

Joan made a noise like a mouse who'd just been trod on. Burke looked startled, then put back his head and laughed. "You came to ask your *sister* about that? Are you mad?"

"Why? What is it?"

Burke laughed again. Douglas began to feel annoyed, but before he could speak, Joan did. "It's a bunch of naughty stories," she said rapidly, "by a very loose woman called Lady Constance. She writes about her lovers and the wicked things they do together. Why on earth do you want to know about them?"

Naughty stories? About the authoress's lovers? Douglas scowled at Burke, who grinned back. "Lady Constance who?" he snapped.

Joan's face was still scarlet. "No one knows. A lady of the *ton*, though; she writes of events that really happened."

"Don't say you've been featured in one of them," her husband added slyly.

Burke was a devil, Douglas thought darkly. He'd enjoyed that facet of his friend's personality more when they were both bachelors. "I don't even know what they are. How could I know if I'd been—?" He stopped as the words sank in. Joan gave a choking sob and buried her face in her hands. "Do you mean *featured*, as one of the lady's lovers?"

"She cuts quite a swath through society, taking home

all sorts of fellows to spend the night in sin." Burke winked. "Sound familiar?"

Joan's shoulders were shaking. Douglas ignored her and glared at Burke. His friend was taking far too much delight in his discomfort. Not that Douglas wouldn't have done the same thing if their positions had been reversed, but he wouldn't have been so openly *gleeful* about it. Of course Douglas wouldn't have asked his sister if he'd known *50 Ways to Sin* was . . . *that*. It could have been a biblical tract for all he knew. But Burke obviously knew and wasn't being the slightest bit discreet about his knowledge, not even with a woman present. The least he could do was answer questions in a straightforward manner, and remember that it was Douglas's sister listening to this, not some trollop.

Douglas chose not to think about said sister's obvious familiarity with the licentious story. No doubt marriage to Burke had corrupted her. "Surely not." He cleared his throat, grasping for a change of subject. "Enough of that. I did have another, more innocent question. I met an intriguing woman last night."

"In which tavern?" drawled Burke, the rotter.

"At the Creighton ball."

"Who?" Joan recovered from her fit enough to uncover her face, although her cheeks were still as red as cherries.

"Madeline Wilde."

Burke shrugged. Joan gaped. "She *spoke* to you?"

"Yes," he said, a bit testily. This visit was not going at all as he had expected, or hoped. "Is that a miracle?"

"Nearly," his sister exclaimed. "She's aloof. Very fashionable, of course—she wore a brilliant gown to the opera last month." An expression of envious rapture settled over her face. "It was simply perfection, with fringed silk trim and rosettes—"

"Who is she?" Douglas knew from experience that his mother and sister could go on for hours about someone's gown and hair and shoes. All he remembered was the way that green silk had draped around Mrs. Wilde's bosom, and how the skirt swayed when she walked. He appreciated her fashion, but not in ways he wanted to discuss with his sister.

Joan looked piqued, but abandoned her praise of Mrs. Wilde's garments. "I don't know much. She's only just respectable. Well, perhaps that's not fair; really it was her mother who was scandalous—Adele Dantes. French, of course. Her husband, Henri Dantes, was a rakehell of truly epic proportions. I daresay he outdid both of you," she added with a coy glance at her husband, who merely winked at her. "But one day he was able to pay off all his debts and no one ever knew how. He gambled and spent just as much as ever until one night he simply fell dead in his tracks of a seizure or some such thing."

"What's the scandal in that?"

"Rumor is that the Duke of Canton paid his debts in exchange for access to Madame Dantes's bed, and that Mrs. Wilde is Canton's natural daughter. I heard one whisper wondering if the duke—or even Madame Dantes herself—might have helped Dantes into his grave. Heaven knows Madame's fortunes improved by staggering bounds after her husband died, even though she never married again. And she's always in the duke's box at the theater." Joan folded her hands primly. "Not that anyone knows anything for certain, of course."

So that's why Spence had called her a courtesan's daughter. "But Mrs. Wilde herself?" he prompted.

"Oh! I don't know much about her. She married respectably enough, to one of the Earl of Carrington's younger sons, but has kept to herself since he died. She's invited everywhere, yet never dances. She seems to know everyone without being friends with anyone. No one ever sees her with a gentleman, except at balls or parties where some men seem to amuse themselves by wagering on who might persuade her to dance." Joan's expression indicated she thought this was his predicament. Douglas didn't move a muscle, not wanting to betray himself that easily. "Mother will have an apoplexy if you chase after her, you know."

He grinned. "Who said I'd have to chase her?"

"Don't be crude," said his sister.

"Just being truthful, sister dear." He got to his feet. "Thank you for the intelligence. I give my word to be discreet in whatever I decide to do with it." He bowed. At the door he paused. "Where might I find one of those stories? I gather Hatchard's isn't the most likely place."

Burke exchanged a look with Joan that made her blush again. "A dusty little bookshop in Madox Street might have it."

For a moment Douglas wondered if he ought to say something to Burke, then decided he didn't actually want to know what went on between his sister and his friend when they were alone. He gave his head a sharp shake to dislodge the thought, and took his leave.

As he made his way to Madox Street, more curious than ever about this mysterious publication, he racked his brains. The Earl of Carrington's son . . . which one could she have married? There were three or four sons there, and after a while he decided it must have been Arthur, the youngest. Douglas had been at Eton with Arthur Wilde, although they'd run in very different circles. Arthur was studious and reserved, a decent chap. Douglas felt a flicker of sorrow for the man. Who wouldn't pity a man who left behind such a wife?

He found the little bookshop without trouble. A bell tinkled as he pushed open the door, and a plump proprietor looked up. "Good day, sir," he said, every syllable well-oiled. "May I help you?"

A quick glance around showed the shop was deserted. "I'm looking for a story called *50 Ways to Sin*."

"I may have an issue or two left—not many, mind you. If you'll pardon me, I'll have a look."

Douglas leaned against the counter as the man disappeared into the back room of the store. Despite Joan's blushes and Burke's sly expression, he found it hard to believe this story would live up to its reputation. How salacious could it be, after all, if Burke let Joan read it? His sister was a well-bred young lady, and Douglas knew his mother had raised her as respectably as possible. Not that it kept Joan from having a streak of independence and daring, but when he thought of the prurient books he'd read, there was no chance this Lady Constance's stories could compare. The poems of the Earl of Rochester had been great favorites among all his mates at university. He amused himself by imagining the swoons and shock Rochester's poetry would cause among the ladies like his sister, and then tried to guess what Lady Constance could write that would make Joan blush so violently. Stolen kisses in a dark garden, most likely, or perhaps some fanciful tale of being kidnapped by a masked highwayman, who would naturally turn out to be a handsome, otherwise honorable gentleman fallen on hard times. If Douglas knew anything about his sister, he knew she liked romance and adventure.

Which only made him wonder again how she'd ended up with Burke, and what the blazes Burke had done to end up with her. Someday he'd force someone to explain that to him.

The shopkeeper came out again, a flat package in his hand. "I apologize for the delay, sir; it had slipped under the shelf. But here it is, and lucky you are to have it. 'Tis my very last copy."

Douglas handed over his coin. "Hard to come by, are they?"

"Quite!" The man chuckled. "Nigh impossible! It's been a fortnight since that one was published, and there's been nary a new issue in sight. I could have sold twice as many."

"Is that so?" Douglas took the package and studied it curiously. "How many did you sell?"

"A great many," said the shopkeeper happily. "It's been very good for business, sir, *very* good."

"Hmm." He slipped the package into his pocket. "Good day."

As soon as he reached his house in Half Moon Street, he tore off the paper. He was still certain it was some overwrought nonsense that appealed to romantic girls, but damn it, he was curious. Someone had offered a bounty for the authoress's name. It made his sister blush fiery red. And it was making that shopkeeper in Madox Street rich. What the devil was this story? Douglas pushed open the door to his sitting room, propped one shoulder against the window frame as he opened the plain, prudish cover, and began to read.

By the end of the first page his eyebrows started to rise.

By the end of the second, his mouth was hanging open.

And when he reached the last page, he no longer cared about Spence's wager or the bounty on Lady Constance's head or what Burke was thinking to let Joan read this. If Madeline Wilde had written this—even if every word sprang solely out of her imagination and not from her experience—he wanted to get to know her much, much better.

# CHAPTER FIVE

Madeline was mildly surprised to see Mr. Bennet head her way two nights after their first meeting. She was a little irritated; a man of his size and looks drew attention, which was the last thing she wanted. He had his eyes fixed on her the whole time, as if he didn't care who knew he was seeking her out, which was also annoying since it made everyone who had turned to watch him swivel around to look at *her*. She kept her faint smile in place, knowing there'd be another rush of rumors about the two of them before dawn tomorrow. Mr. Bennet was proving difficult to put in his place.

Still, as he drew nearer, the crowd now parting in front of him as if to give her a good look, a little jolt of something else shot through her. Not irritation, not annoyance, not surprise. She supposed she wouldn't be a woman if she didn't get a shock of . . . awareness. That was it, *awareness*, not interest or even worse, attraction. He had adopted the strictest fashion and wore all black except for his waistcoat and cravat, and the effect was quite devastating. It highlighted how very trim and athletic his figure was, broad shouldered and fit. He'd combed his thick auburn hair back from his face, banishing the mussed romantic appearance of the last time she'd seen him. And his hazel eyes were fixed on her with an intensity that ought to have irked her but somehow, instead, made her heart skip a beat.

"Mrs. Wilde." He bowed when he reached her.

"Good evening, sir. What have you wagered this evening?"

"Nothing," he said easily. He plucked two glasses from a footman's tray and handed her one. "As you guessed when first we met, I lost last time, and I hate losing. Tonight I've only come for my own pleasure."

She arched one brow. "With no thought to mine?"

"No, I thought a great deal about your pleasure as well." His eyes warmed, but he didn't steal a glance at her bosom, as so many men did. He seemed fascinated by her face. "About our mutual pleasure."

Madeline took a sip of champagne to hide her flinch. She was fairly disgusted with herself for letting him have any effect on her, let alone such an overtly physical one. "Perhaps my pleasure does not involve you at all. Perhaps my pleasure is for you to go away and leave me in peace."

"So you can stand here and watch in solitude?" He shook his head and propped one shoulder against the pillar beside her. "Where's the pleasure in that?"

She didn't attend balls for pleasure. She attended to hear the latest gossip and the freshest scandals, which were vital to her work for Liam. If she danced and drank, she'd never keep the rumors straight, and besides, a reputation for aloofness seemed to lead to more invitations, not fewer. Tonight she barely knew the host and hostess. Madeline supposed she was invited because she was an enigma: a fashionable woman with connections, but also with a whiff of scandal clinging to her. An independent woman who lived a comfortable life with no apparent means of support. There were never enough wealthy widows to satisfy the penniless rakes and rogues who prowled the drawing rooms of Mayfair in pursuit of fresh prey.

"You have no idea what gives me pleasure," she told him. She had no doubt his attentions were focused on getting her into bed and little more.

"But I'm here to learn," he said, flashing his heart-stopping grin. "We can begin from the beginning." He smoothed his cravat and cleared his throat. "Good evening, ma'am. Are you enjoying the party?"

She had to smile. "Tolerably."

"Tolerably!" He frowned. "What a poor comment on our hostess's taste. Is it the music? I like a good reel myself, none of this quadrille. Who dances the quadrille anymore? It always brings to mind my grandmother, who was the most accomplished quadrille partner I've ever known, although it would have pained me to admit it at age twelve, when she patiently taught me the steps."

"Perhaps you have forgotten how seductive and romantic a quadrille can be."

He paused, with a distant expression, then shook his head. "No, I really saw nothing seductive or romantic about it. The fact that I remember my grandmother as my favorite partner proves that."

"A reel is hardly more so. It allows no time for conversation or intrigue."

"No," he agreed with a laugh. "But it's a rollicking good

time, and I like that about a dance. If one wants to talk, it's better to find a quiet moment to focus all one's attention on the other person." His admiring gaze moved over her face again. "Such as now."

Madeline told herself he was just flirting, but it was hard not to enjoy it. Even though he was distracting her from her object—from her livelihood—she couldn't bring herself to be cold and withering. "But we have nothing to talk about," she said gently. "You have no wager, I have no interest in dancing. After we discuss the weather, we'll have nothing else to say and this quiet moment, as you call it, will grow awkward and tiresome."

"That's unfair. How do you know I haven't got a list of things to discuss with you?" He nodded at her start of surprise. "I learned it early: Never approach a lady without some prepared topic of conversation. It eliminates the risk of that awkward silence. And if things should progress to a more natural and easy conversation, so much the better."

He was making her want to laugh. "I see. What topics were you prepared to discuss with me, then?"

"Dancing, obviously," he said. "That bit about my grandmother is absolutely true. She was bent on teaching me proper dances and rapped my knuckles when I tried to dodge the lessons. Once, to punish me, she let my sister watch." He shook his head, looking grim. "It was a lasting humiliation." Madeline found herself smiling, and quickly took another sip of champagne. He sighed and gave a shrug. "Do you not dance out of choice, or are you unable?"

She choked. "Unable?"

He nodded seriously. "For all I know, you've got a peg leg. That would make it dashed hard to waltz about or skip through a reel."

"I have not got a peg leg!"

He seemed oblivious to her indignation. "Or perhaps you don't know how. It's not a sin. In fact, it's more likely to be a sin to enjoy dancing, so not knowing might be counted a virtue." His engaging grin flashed again. "But I wouldn't know; virtue isn't my strength."

She had to cough to cover her laugh this time. "Mr. Bennet. I know very well how to dance, thank you, and I have all my limbs in good health. Choosing not to dance with the scoundrels and rogues who ask me is a perfectly sound decision, and not reflective of virtue or vice."

"Ah . . . I see. So which am I: scoundrel or rogue?"

"Pardon?" She blinked.

"I asked you to dance and you refused." He nodded once. "Therefore I must be a scoundrel or a rogue, by your estimation. I was curious to which camp you assigned me."

"I—" She pressed her lips together. "Rogue."

His eyes lit up. "Rogue! May I ask how you determined it?"

"Scoundrels are dishonest at heart. Rogues are merely careless of others' feelings and sensibilities."

Instead of being offended, he clapped one hand to his chest and gave a great sigh. "I'm so relieved. Scoundrel has such a bad air about it, doesn't it? Rather like a fellow who would ask a woman to marry him and then not arrive at the church, or some such thing. A rogue, though, sounds very dashing. I imagine he has a splendid pair of horses and drives a smart phaeton around the park, tipping his hat to the ladies—*all* the ladies, mind you."

"You seem well informed about the species." Madeline realized she'd finished her champagne. Pity; she only allowed herself one glass a night, and she barely remembered sipping this one.

He nodded. "I have a great many friends, and most of them are scoundrels or rogues." He took the empty glass from her hand, neatly switching it with a fresh one on a footman's tray. He handed it to her without a word. She knew she should protest, but somehow didn't say anything. "I never quite knew how to categorize them until now, and for that I thank you."

"I am sure it's kept you awake at nights."

"One or two," he said with a long-suffering expression. "A night of dancing, though, always sends me right to sleep." Again his sly, coaxing grin. "If you should change your mind about dancing, I would happily oblige."

She gave him a wry glance. "Perhaps I refused because I simply didn't wish to dance with you."

"Why wouldn't you?" he exclaimed. "I'm a cracking good dancer, I'll have you know."

"How could I know that?" She gestured with one hand. "Dance with someone else and I shall see for myself how accomplished you are."

He leaned a little closer to her. "If I didn't know better, I'd think that was a ploy to get rid of me."

"Ploy?" Madeline opened her eyes very wide. "I thought

it was only a shade more subtle than saying, 'Please go away, Mr. Bennet.'"

"Just a shade." He turned and surveyed the ballroom. "What will it earn me if I dance with someone else? I've no real desire of my own to do it, so you must convince me."

"Surely you can't wish to remain in this lonely corner with me," she said lightly. "A handsome gentleman of good fortune who is an excellent dancer? Do not let your talents languish in obscurity, sir."

He shook his head almost regretfully. "The very fact that you admit I'm handsome makes me want to stay here all the more. Try again."

She let out a breath of amused frustration, and took a sip of champagne. "You may find someone more interested in your charm."

"Now I sense a challenge. You think I'm charming."

Madeline's gaze narrowed. "Please go away, Mr. Bennet."

He laughed. "Enough with politeness! Very well. I will go away and dance with every woman here who'll have me, if only . . ." He propped his arm against the pillar above her head, angling even closer. Madeline took a fortifying breath to keep herself from leaning back, away from the heat and scent of him. "If you let me drive you home tonight."

"I don't need—"

He put one fingertip on her lips, stopping her retort. "Who said anything of need? Agree that I shall drive you home tonight, and I'll leave you in peace the rest of the evening. And before you doubt my intentions, I promise on my grandmother's memory that I shan't even think of entering your door. I will see you safely home and go on my way. I'm a rogue, remember, not a scoundrel." He winked, which combined with the intimate smile on his face to make her knees feel a little weak and her heart skip a beat.

She tried to calm her irrational reaction and think of her own interest. No one would bother her if he escorted her home. If he tried to charm his way inside, Constance would be waiting with the pistol. And it was a short drive to her house from here. She could endure that in exchange for a respite from his overpowering presence for the rest of the evening. "Done," she said in a low voice.

His eyes darkened. "We have a pact." He caught her hand and raised it to his lips, barely brushing her knuckles. "Signal me when you are ready to leave. Until then, madam, farewell." He released her hand and sauntered away without a backward glance.

When he left, the temperature around her seemed to drop several degrees. She told herself that was good, as she'd felt increasingly hot and flustered by his proximity, but she still tipped her glass to her lips and washed down the rest of her champagne. With a mental shake, she put the glass on a nearby table and tried to clear her mind. She had work to do tonight, and so far the evening had been a total loss because of Douglas Bennet.

Well . . . not, perhaps, a total loss. She watched him move among the other guests, chatting easily with men and bringing simpering smiles to the faces of the ladies. After several minutes, he led out the widowed Countess of Farnham. Madeline pressed her lips together; the countess was a beautiful woman, and her blond hair looked very striking next to Mr.

Bennet's auburn head. She caught a glimpse of the woman's face as they moved through the bagatelle. Lady Farnham was very pleased to be in his arms, and unless Madeline missed her guess very badly, she'd be glad to stay there all night long.

With great effort she looked away. *The infamous Mr. B, long a favorite of the ladies of London,* she mentally composed. *But this night he devoted himself solely to one lady.* That would serve him right for walking away so quickly, she thought, and then wondered why she was jealous. She'd told him to walk away.

She tried not to watch him for the next two hours. True to his word, he never came near her. She was only able to glean a few tidbits of gossip—everyone here seemed determined to be wretchedly respectable—but she also noticed that Mr. Bennet danced with six ladies. Three were widows, two were unhappily married, and one was a rather lovely heiress. Madeline hesitated to insert the name of any unmarried lady into her writing without ironclad proof of scandalous behavior, but she was very tempted when she saw Miss Margaret Childress, only child of a wealthy banker, in his arms, smiling with less than her usual coyness.

When Madeline was ready to leave, she raised her hand. Although he was still dancing with Mrs. Powell, a general's wife with a roving eye, Mr. Bennet gave her a brief nod. At the end of the dance, he escorted his partner from the floor. From where Madeline stood, the lady didn't seem eager for him to leave her; she maintained her grip on his arm, leaning closer and tilting her head in unmistakable invitation. Her eyelashes fluttered as she spoke to him. And he smiled back at her, laying his hand over hers on his arm.

Well. Surely that released her from their bargain. She wasn't even sure why she'd considered herself bound by it at all. She'd have done much better to leave while he was distracted by Mrs. Powell's impressive bosom. Madeline stalked toward the door. She certainly wasn't going to stand around waiting while he arranged his rendezvous for later. In the hall she asked a servant to bring her cloak, telling herself the pounding of her heart was from relief at the reprieve she'd just been given and not from any lingering desire to hear his footsteps behind her.

"Here we are." His voice made her jump, and then he was draping her cloak over her shoulders. "I hope you weren't waiting long."

"I wasn't waiting," she replied.

"I gave my word." He put on his hat and gloves. He must have sent the footman running to fetch them so quickly. "As did you."

She pursed her lips. "I gave my word that you could drive me home. I never vowed to wait for you if you were otherwise engaged when I wished to leave."

"If you're trying to wriggle out of it, don't bother." He offered his arm. "I'm persistent."

"That's not always an admirable quality."

"No, often not," he agreed, leading her out to a waiting carriage. "But I was determined to know your judgment on my dancing. Where are we going?"

She hesitated, but there was no dodging it. "Brunswick Square, number eight."

He told the driver and helped her into the carriage. His

hand engulfed hers. Madeline tried to confine herself to a small portion of the seat, but he still seemed to fill the carriage. His arm bumped hers as he sat down; goodness, his shoulders were broad. She shouldn't have agreed to this. It was easy to brush him off in a crowded, public ballroom. Now there was no way she could avoid the scent of him, the warmth of his body next to hers, or the way he looked at her as the carriage rocked forward.

"Are you impressed?"

She blinked. Had her thoughts been that obvious?

"I danced six times, more than enough to judge my skill." He gave her a sinful glance. "I am breathlessly awaiting your verdict."

She took an unsteady breath. "Very accomplished."

He nodded once in satisfaction. "I told you. It's very much your loss if you don't dance with me now."

Madeline laughed. "It certainly is."

"So if you haven't got a peg leg and you admit I'm the finest dancer you've ever seen, why do you stand at the back of the room and turn aside my every invitation?"

"You flatter yourself, sir," she murmured.

"Do I?" He twisted in his seat to look at her more directly. "I saw your face while I waltzed with Lady Farnham. I recognize envy when I see it."

"Lady Farnham wore a very beautiful gown tonight," Madeline replied. "I believe every woman there envied her."

"I hear your fashion is also quite enviable."

"You don't seem the sort to care about fashion."

He lifted one shoulder. Madeline tried not to shiver as

it brushed hers again. "I appreciate how a woman looks. It doesn't depend on what sort of fringe her gown has, though."

"You underestimate the power of fringe."

Mr. Bennet laughed. "I doubt it. Although . . ." He delicately touched one of the emerald ribbons on her cloak. "This does make your eyes look very green."

She looked at him. His entire attention was fixed on her, and even in the dark carriage she felt exposed. "My eyes are brown, not green," she managed to whisper.

"No, they're not," he murmured. He leaned closer, angling his head to peer deep into her eyes . . . or as though he might kiss her. Madeline sat frozen, unable to retreat and somehow not outraged enough to slap his face. "Most of the time they're brown, but when you laugh or smile, they sparkle with glints of gold and green. I quite like the golden glints."

"I doubt you can see any of that now." Her voice was appallingly husky.

Slowly he shook his head. "I don't need light to see them. I dreamt of them all last night." Without taking his gaze from her face, he opened the carriage door. "Here we are."

Madeline's eyelids closed as he climbed down. She hadn't even realized the carriage had stopped. She really needed to heed Liam's warning and stay away from this man. He helped her down and walked her to her door, waiting as she took out her key. "Thank you for escorting me, sir." On no account was she letting him inveigle an invitation inside, not even for a moment.

But as she braced herself for it, he stepped back and touched the brim of his hat. "It was my pleasure, Mrs. Wilde."

He walked to the carriage without another word. Madeline concentrated on the lock and let herself in. As she was closing the door behind her, she caught one last glimpse of him, still standing and watching, still focused on her with an intensity that left her unsettled.

Oh dear. What had she done?

# CHAPTER SIX

Spence found him the following morning at the boxing saloon.

Douglas saw him at the back of the room, leaning on his walking stick and smiling in his smug way. Since he was standing in the ring at the moment, sparring with an opponent, he chose to ignore Spence. There were no bouts in progress, nor any planned for the day, which meant there was precious little to wager on. There was a chance Spence would grow bored and leave, and Douglas wouldn't have to see him for another day. That thought made him realize he'd been unconsciously avoiding Spence while he plotted how he could see Madeline Wilde again and win her over . . . and that thought distracted him enough to take a hard jab in the stomach.

His sparring partner, Sir Philip Albright, stopped short as he doubled over. "Damn, Bennet, did I hurt you?"

He waved one hand as he staggered around the ring, trying to catch his breath. Spence was almost laughing at him now, the blighter. "Not a bit. My fault. Again?" He threw himself back into the bout and refocused his attention on the pressing matter at hand, namely beating Albright for landing a blow that would hurt like the devil tomorrow.

Afterward he beat a retreat to the changing room, where he knew a dandy like Spence wouldn't follow. He took his time washing up and getting dressed, trying not to think about why he wasn't simply facing down the man. He didn't owe Spence anything; he had nothing to fear. In fact, now he was better informed than before, which ought to lend him an advantage in the confrontation.

Douglas scowled at the mirror as he knotted his cravat roughly. He didn't like Spence anymore. Had he ever, really? Spence was always willing to lend a mate some blunt, and he was always up for a night in the gaming hells or brothels. But Douglas knew what Spence wanted to discuss, and he wasn't in the mood. The truth was, he was beginning to like Mrs. Wilde. If she was really Lady Constance, he wanted to know—but for himself, not for some bloody bounty.

With a final curse under his breath, he grabbed his jacket and strode through the saloon, right at Spence. "Fancy a round?" He hoped the man would say yes. A good sparring bout was invigorating, and the thought of punching him had grown appealing.

Slender and elegant, Spence wrinkled his nose. "Of course not. I have an eye for choosing winning fighters, not for throwing punches myself."

"Odd place to hang about, then, given there's no fight going on."

The other man smirked. "How are you getting on with our little wager?"

Douglas put on his jacket and took his hat from the boy

who ran after him. "The one about the Ascot? You may take Grafton's filly after her performance at The Oaks. I wouldn't stake two shillings on her."

"Not the racing wager," said Spence, still smiling. "The Wilde wager."

Douglas tugged on his gloves as he went out the door. "I managed to find a copy of the story you mentioned. Don't you think it's strange that Chesterton would want to dissuade people he's the man in it—Lord Masterly?"

"I don't give a bleeding damn, I only want his money."

Spence looked vaguely like a weasel sometimes, Douglas thought. "Of course, but what if he doesn't intend to pay? The lady praises him in rather intimate detail. She's quite complimentary, in fact, about his prowess and endowment and even his generosity, which is not how most people think of Chesterton. He's a pompous prig and no one would guess he's a good lover to look at him." Spence frowned. "If you ask me," Douglas added, "I think he announced a bounty to draw attention to it, and cause a little stir about his unexpected talents. Is he on the outs with his mistress?"

He'd made an impression. Spence didn't reply, and his frown grew deeper. What a coup; it was rare Douglas ever felt the thrill of outsmarting anyone, and he allowed himself a momentary bit of pride.

It faded quickly, though. Spence took a deep breath and smiled again, this time colder and more reptilian than ever. "Perhaps. I don't care why he announced a bounty. I only care that he's done it publicly, which means he shall be forced to pay if you succeed in exposing Mrs. Wilde."

"Only if she's the author," Douglas reminded him. "She may not be."

"We agreed to split the bounty if *you* proved her guilty before anyone else did," Spence replied. His humor seemed fully restored now, and his parting words only squashed what was left of Douglas's good mood. "Did you really think I'd leave it entirely in your hands? I like to spread my chances around. Good day, Bennet." Smiling broadly now, he tipped his head and walked away.

# CHAPTER SEVEN

After another long night—made longer by her inability to stop thinking about Douglas Bennet saying he'd dreamt of her—Madeline slept late. It didn't help. She still woke feeling restless and cross. *That man*, she fumed as Constance brushed out her hair. That man was making a nuisance of himself. For a moment she wished he'd be rude or impertinent, or baldly ask her to go to bed with him. Then she could reject him and he could leave in a fit of petulance. She didn't like his flirting, and she really didn't like his serious conversation, when he claimed there were glints of gold in her eyes. He was a rogue, and despite what she'd told him, rogues were just as bad as scoundrels in her book. The fact that he seemed delighted to be called one only reflected poorly on his character. And if he would stop being charming she would be able to banish him without hesitation.

She started when Mr. Nash jumped into her lap. "I thought you'd gone out," she told the cat, stroking his back. He purred at her, circling until he found a position he liked, with his front paws tucked between her knees and his tail swishing against her hip. Madeline rolled her eyes but continued petting him.

"He didn't want out this morning, madam." Constance ran the brush through her hair once more. "Shall I leave it down, or will you be going out?"

Madeline glanced at the clock. It was nearly noon. The sun shone outside and a warm breeze blew through the open window. She wasn't pleased with her writing last night, but instead of staying in to work on it, she wanted to get out of the house. "No, I'm going out."

She put on her favorite walking dress. Only when Constance was doing the final buttons did she notice the fabric made her eyes look almost green. She leaned closer to the mirror, squinting, and then straightened with a huff. Perhaps there *were* small streaks of green in her eyes. How odd she'd never noticed them before. And how much odder that he had.

Mr. Nash bounded down the stairs ahead of her as she went, winding his way around her feet as she tugged on her gloves. Constance shooed the cat away and fetched a shawl. "I'll be a few hours," Madeline told the maid, putting on her bonnet. "Tell Mrs. Robbins something light for dinner tonight. I'll dine at home." Mrs. Robbins was the woman who came in every other day to cook. Madeline went out so often during the Season, she had no need for a live-in cook.

Constance nodded. "Yes, madam."

"And keep Mr. Nash out of it. A cat must not eat lobster soup." She shook a scolding finger at the cat, who retaliated by rubbing his face against her shoe, purring hard. Unwillingly she smiled. "You're too charming for your own good." He draped himself over her feet, and she gave in, scooping him up and letting him butt his head beneath her chin. Madeline sighed even as she held him like a baby. "I cannot believe I'm so softhearted with you."

"Like all men," remarked Constance. "He's handsome and knows how to melt a woman's heart to get himself out of trouble." She loved the cat almost as much as Madeline did. It was probably Constance's fault Mr. Nash was so spoiled.

She snorted with amusement and put her pet down. "How true. But no lobster soup for him."

"I'll do my best, madam." Constance grinned as the cat transferred his attentions to her hem, where a loose thread hung down. He took a swipe with one paw, then with the other. "Faithless little beast. Already distracted by another woman's skirt."

Madeline laughed and opened the door as Mr. Nash made another leap at the thread. Distracted by the cat's antics, she took a step out before registering that someone stood at the bottom of her steps. "Mr. Bennet," she exclaimed.

He bowed slightly. "Mrs. Wilde."

She'd only seen him in candlelit ballrooms, and last night, by the glow of the moon. In the full light of day he was dazzling. His hair shone like polished mahogany as he doffed his hat. His shoulders seemed broader than ever, his figure more athletic. His eyes lit up as he smiled. Madeline was struck speechless for a moment as he rested one booted foot on the first step and leaned forward.

"I was just about to knock," he said. "And then you appeared as if in answer to my prayer."

With some small effort she shook off her daze. "You must not waste your prayers on something so mundane."

"Never question a man's relationship with Almighty God," he returned. "I cannot think of anything less mundane than the sight of you."

"You haven't tried very hard, if that's true."

"No," he cheerfully admitted. "Once I start thinking of you, I don't try to think of anything else." He extended his right arm, which had been behind his back. A small but lovely bouquet of pale yellow roses was in his hand. "In fact, thoughts of you struck me very forcibly as I was passing a flower seller, and I was compelled to bring you these."

Madeline blinked, off balance. No one had brought her flowers since Arthur died. None of the rogues and scoundrels who sidled up to her in ballrooms ever tried to call on her. "Thank you," she said. "They're lovely." She took the bouquet, then wished she hadn't. It implied an acceptance of his attentions, which were not turning out to be as transient as she'd promised Liam. "How kind of you to deliver them yourself."

He grinned. "Yes, wasn't it?"

The polite thing would be to invite him inside. Madeline resisted it. That was a line she would not cross, not for him or for any other man. "I didn't expect such solicitousness." She turned to her maid. "Constance, please put these in a vase."

Constance was watching from behind her with unabashed interest. Madeline could tell from her expression that Mr. Bennet had impressed her greatly—or at least his figure had. At Madeline's words, she tore her eyes off him and took the roses. "Yes, madam." Somewhat reluctantly she went into the house, almost tripping over Mr. Nash as she went.

Madeline turned back to her caller, who still stood on her steps looking unbearably attractive. "I was about to go out, sir. I beg your pardon for being unable to converse longer." She closed the door firmly behind her.

He didn't move. "Nonsense. You needn't beg my pardon, for you couldn't have known I would call at this moment unless you were watching from your window for me." He paused with a hopeful glance. "I don't suppose you were, were you?"

"Certainly not."

Mr. Bennet gave a nod. "Then it's only a happy coincidence."

She blinked. Happy?

His grin deepened into something more sensual. "Now I can offer my escort on your walk."

She should have seen that coming. Unfortunately her wits seemed to desert her when he was around. "I— How do you know I plan to walk?"

"There's no carriage waiting. It's a splendid day. And now that you have a handsome and charming escort at hand, you can hardly refuse."

"Perhaps I wanted solitude," she tried. "Perhaps you don't wish to walk as far as I intend."

His eyebrows went up. "Do you plan to go to Hampstead Heath?"

She shook her head, and from the corner of her eye caught sight of another man, lingering at the edge of the square. He wasn't even facing her way but something about his pose brought back the sensation of being watched and followed. A chill whispered up her spine. She was probably being silly, and yet . . . Perhaps an escort wasn't a bad idea, even an escort as distracting as Mr. Bennet.

"No, Mr. Bennet, I plan to walk to Bond Street."

"That's a long walk." He fell back as she came down the steps.

"On such a splendid day?" She smiled without looking at him. "I look forward to the exercise."

He set his hat back on his head and fell in beside her. "I'm very fond of exercise, too."

She couldn't resist a covert glance at him. It was obvious. He was exceedingly fit. "Of walking?"

He laughed. "Among other things." There was a wealth of meaning in his tone, and she cursed herself. "I spent the morning at the boxing saloon, and I find a brisk walk afterward helps restore my balance."

An image of him stripped to the waist and gleaming with sweat popped into her mind. Madeline fought desperately to think of any other subject. "And you found yourself all the way here. Your balance must be very shaken."

He walked beside her without offering his arm, for which she was grateful. It was bad enough being close to him, hearing the low rumble of his laugh, seeing for herself how very strong and male he was. She couldn't forget how unsettling it had been to share a carriage seat with him. If she had to lean on his arm as well, and feel how firm and muscled he was . . .

"I don't believe I've ever been more shaken, Mrs. Wilde." She turned her head sharply. He spoke lightly and yet there was something in his words that made her think he meant something other than balance. "Perhaps you'd be so good as to take my arm, in case I feel unsteady."

"Perhaps you should hail a carriage," she said. "You ought not to risk your health, sir."

He made a soft regretful *tsk.* "I didn't see a single carriage for hire as I walked here."

"I'd wager we shall find one within a few streets."

"I'll take that wager," he said at once. "If we don't see a carriage before Bloomsbury Square, you must take my arm."

Madeline couldn't imagine there wouldn't be a single hackney before then. Still, it was a risk. They had reached Russell Square, a quiet neighborhood. If she lost she'd have to wrap her hand around his strong arm and walk very close to him . . . "Very well." Fortunately, less than two minutes later, they turned a corner and she spied a hackney carriage ahead, stopped at the watering trough. "You lose, Mr. Bennet," she said with a tinge of relief. "I see a hackney standing there." The driver was adjusting the harness; it was obviously available for hire.

Disappointment flickered over his face. "Well played, Mrs. Wilde." He clasped his hands behind his back.

"This is home to me," she reminded him. "I walk these streets often."

"Yes, I did suspect that. Why?" At her frown, he went on. "It's quite a cozy part of town but it's really not safe for a lady to walk alone."

"I'm not alone."

"No," he said in a low, intimate voice. "Not today."

Madeline realized she had strayed closer to his side. She made herself move away. "What do you want from me, Mr. Bennet?"

Again he tilted his head to look at her, his expression thoughtful. "I like you," he said after a moment. "I would like to know you better."

"Why?"

"You're intriguing."

"I am not," she said immediately. Liam's words echoed in her mind; perhaps she shouldn't have been so quick to refuse his help. She still didn't feel frightened of Douglas Bennet, but he had turned up at her house, and she shouldn't like that. She *didn't* like that, she told herself.

"To me you are."

"Because I won't dance with you?"

"Well, that *is* quite shocking," he agreed. "And after you noted how well I dance!"

"I also noted you're a rogue."

"My saving grace," he said with a wink. "But how can you claim to know what intrigues me? You don't know me, either, aside from a bit of gossip."

Madeline smiled. When they first met, she'd meant to set him back on his heels. He was surprising her, though. "Ah yes. In which particular was I wrong? Have you lost your family fortune? Or perhaps you've reconsidered your preference for opera dancers?"

"The family fortune is intact," he said. "And you do wrong by opera dancers. They take their dancing very seriously, which adds inestimably to the performance. Surely you don't mean to deny the girls a chance to make a living by their talents?"

That needle struck home, though she couldn't let him know it. "Of course not," she said in exaggerated indignation. "Judge not, that you be not judged. I adhere very firmly to this maxim."

"Do you?" He gave her a meaningful glance. "Always?"

"Was I unfair to you? Was anything I said incorrect?"

"You said I pitied my friend for wedding my sister, and that is untrue." He paused. "I was very surprised by it, but I wish them both great happiness."

She shot him a quick glance, but there was no wryness in his tone, and his expression was easy and open. It pricked her conscience that she had dismissed him so blithely. "But the rest?"

"Absolutely spot-on," he said at once. "I am without a doubt a brilliant dancer, as well as handsome, charming, and fond of the occasional wager."

She laughed. That was another mark against him: he made her laugh even when she knew she should brush him off and give him the cut direct if he approached her again.

"Now," he went on, his voice dropping to that seductive register, "I expect all this walking has made you very hungry. Shall I treat you to an ice at Gunter's?"

"I'm not hungry."

"How can you not be? I'm half starved from all this exercise."

Madeline knew he wasn't serious. Far from weakened, he strolled along beside her, easily keeping the brisk pace she set. If anything, she felt a little hot and breathless while he wasn't even flushed. "I will understand if you must stop at a tavern to revive your flagging strength."

They had reached Oxford Street, where the traffic was heavy and steady. Her companion gave her a dangerous smile as he turned his head toward her. "My strength isn't flagging in the slightest. Everything about you invigorates me. And I could show you. In fact . . . I would be very, very pleased to do so."

"Unlike you, sir, I take people at their word. If you aren't fatigued, I believe it." It was a very good retort, she told herself—or it would have been if she had managed to deliver it in anything approaching a cool and composed manner, instead of in a breathless, almost husky voice. From the way his eyes warmed as he smiled down at her, he had taken more meaning from her tone than from her words.

"I wish you would take me at my word," he murmured. "I've never lied to you, and I never will."

"Never?" Another word she'd meant to say archly, even tartly, but instead had whispered with a hopeful, wondering lilt.

And again, he reacted to that. His smile faded and his fingers tightened around hers. "Never," he promised.

A wagon rumbled past, so near the horse's tail nearly brushed her skirts as it swished from side to side. In the blink of an eye Mr. Bennet spun her around, almost lifting her off her feet as he moved between her and the traffic. She clutched at him for balance, too startled to speak. No one had done that since Arthur died. She'd got used to looking after herself and keeping everyone else, especially gentlemen, at bay. It was only this gentleman who refused to be kept at arm's length—whom she had trouble *remembering* to keep at arm's length.

"Sorry," said Mr. Bennet. "Are you all right?"

Only then did she realize that his arm had gone around her waist, and his hand to her shoulder. Given the way she was still clinging to his coat, they were nearly in each other's arms, right on the side of Oxford Street in the middle of the day. And instead of being uncomfortable at the public display or appalled at her own lack of discipline, she felt a deep throb of longing in her chest. She hadn't felt that since Arthur's death, either. "Yes," she said lamely. "I'm perfectly fine."

He didn't release her. Nor did she release him. "It's disgraceful how people drive in London," he said.

"Yes." Her heart hammered. With some effort she pried her fingers loose from his clothing. "Thank you."

For a moment he just looked down at her, as if she'd caught him off guard; his gaze was clear and a little startled. His lips parted, but then his arms fell away and he stepped back. "Now I insist on taking you for an ice. It's the least I can do in apology for seizing you like that."

She felt an unaccountable blush warm her face and dropped her gaze. It landed on his boots, now heavily spattered with mud. She blinked and glanced at her skirt, not surprised to see a few splashes of the same on her hem. When she looked up, Mr. Bennet had noticed.

"My sister would be in despair if her favorite dress got so dirty," he said with a rueful look. "I should have paid more attention to the reckless idiots racing up Oxford Street. It was my fault for leading you right to the edge of the street."

"Your boots are much dirtier," she pointed out.

He shrugged. "Leather cleans up better than cloth."

"How did you know this is my favorite dress?"

His gaze drifted down, then back up until it met her own. "How could it not be? It makes your eyes glow."

Madeline had a terrible feeling that his company was far more to blame for that. "It's just a dress," she murmured.

He offered his arm again. "And they're just boots."

They were expensive boots of fine leather. It was a small act of chivalry, the sort any number of men might have performed. But the fact remained that only Douglas Bennet had; only he persisted in the face of her cool attempts to rebuff him. Only he charmed his way through her defenses until she had to admit, to herself if not to him, that she liked his company. She liked the spark of awareness that went through her when he appeared. She liked the way he made her laugh despite all her resolve not to—in fact, she liked laughing again. It had been a long time since she'd done so as frequently and as easily as she had with him.

This time she took his arm without demur. This time she let her steps stray close to his side until his elbow brushed her waist and she could smell the vibrant scent of his soap. This time . . .

This time she let herself hope he was in earnest when he said he wanted to get to know her better.

## CHAPTER EIGHT

For once Douglas had nothing to say.

It had seemed a fairly ordinary thing, swinging Madeline Wilde away from the wagon about to splash muck on them. His father would have done the same for his mother, and Burke would probably shield Joan as well. It was an ordinary, gentlemanly thing to do.

And now he knew exactly how she felt in his arms, and how beautiful she was when she wasn't trying to run him off. For that moment there, when he held her close and she held tight to him, he'd had the strongest feeling of . . . awe.

If only he knew what it really meant, and how he ought to respond. As thrilling as it was to flirt with her, he did want more. Unfortunately he didn't know how one went about pursuing *more* with a woman. His expertise was in flirting and charming, not in pursuing a more serious or lasting relationship. He didn't even know what he wanted—more than a flirtation, more than a brief affair, but surely not anything . . . irrevocable.

*Irrevocable* meant marriage, and Douglas was not a marrying man. He liked barmaids and opera dancers, the sort of women who would never expect a man of his position to marry them. He stole a sideways glance at Mrs. Wilde. No tavern wench could hold a candle to her, with her faintly accented voice and mysterious smile and golden curls he was desperate to see streaming loose around her bare shoulders. She was a widow, he argued to himself, an independent woman; she probably didn't want anything irrevocable, either. She hadn't even agreed to dance with him yet, for God's sake. She knew very well he wanted her, and he could tell she found him attractive. It was only a matter of time and persistence before they ended up in bed together. He'd never been so determined to make a woman like him. Once he succeeded— once she began to crave his company the way he did hers—he would show her how attentive and devoted he could be. It would take him years to enact all the fantasies he'd had about her, and once he had her in his arms, wild and eager, he'd make damned sure she never wanted to leave.

But wait. He stopped those thoughts in alarm. If she never wanted to leave him and he never wanted to leave her, that sounded . . . permanent. Permanent was only a short leap from irrevocable.

Good God, was this what had happened to Burke? Once upon a time Burke had regarded Joan as the greatest Fury in London—or so he'd said. He'd called her trouble and said he meant to avoid her. Douglas had even felt guilty imposing on his friend by asking him to keep an eye on his sister when he and his parents had left London. And yet a month later Joan was married to Burke. There must have been something scandalous to prompt it, although Burke had weathered plenty of scandals without batting an eye, let alone getting married. No one in Douglas's acquaintance was more daring, more immune to matrimony, more careless of propriety than Burke . . . but no one had had to march him to the church at sword point, either. Burke had been there pacing the aisle when Douglas arrived, in fact, as if he couldn't wait for the ceremony. And after his visit to Hanover Square the other day, Douglas could tell his friend was pleased with his lot. If a hell-raiser like Burke could slip and get caught in the bonds of marriage, it could happen to anyone.

Couldn't it?

He glanced at Mrs. Wilde again. Did she hold him at bay because she wanted marriage? People whispered about her, but mostly about her air of unattainability. Joan said the only scandal was connected to her vaguely suspect parentage. Spence had called her the courtesan's daughter, but she had steadfastly resisted his every effort to charm her. Hell, it had taken over a week of determined effort to get her to take his arm and walk with him.

Mrs. Wilde indicated a shop she needed to visit. He held the door for her, then hung back and pretended to examine a display of quills, but the stationer's shop was small. There was no way to avoid overhearing her order a large quantity of paper and several bottles of ink, to be delivered to her home. From the shopkeeper's manner, Douglas sensed this was a typical order for her.

It made him think of Spence's stupid wager. Why did she need that much paper? Not even Douglas's mother, who seemed to have a vast network of gossipy friends all over Britain, wrote enough letters to need so much. And Mrs. Wilde didn't order fine pressed paper, suitable for letters, but coarser sheets, the sort one wouldn't mind throwing on the fire if the writer was displeased with her work.

"You must be planning to write a novel," he said as they left the shop.

Her dark eyes flashed his way. "You don't strike me as the sort to care much about novels."

Douglas grinned. "Very true. I never was one for books."

She smiled. "But what a world you've missed! Novels are the form that makes history feel familiar and real, the vehicle for science and philosophy to become human. They cannot compare to books assigned by a tutor or professor."

"I didn't want to take the risk, so avoided them all." He cocked his head to see her face. She had taken his arm this time without any protest, and he liked the feel of her beside him. If he could make her laugh, he'd count this entire day a victory. "So you *are* writing a novel?"

Her mouth curved as if at some secret joke. "No."

Curse Spence. Without that bounty, Douglas wouldn't have noticed if she ordered enough paper to print the *London Gazette* for a year. On the other hand, if Spence hasn't dared him to do it, he might never have made such a point of seeking her out. He decided to reserve judgment for a while longer. "Poetry?" he guessed again. "A play?"

"Neither."

"Have you got a printing press in your sitting room?" he asked with a laugh.

She whipped around. "What?"

"You've bought enough paper to publish your own newspaper every week."

She blinked, then gave a laugh of her own. Her fingers twitched on his arm. "How ridiculous!"

Douglas's grin faded, belatedly realizing she'd been too startled. What did that mean? She couldn't really be printing *50 Ways to Sin* herself. And yet . . . that would help explain why no one had been able to trace the pamphlets. A shadow fell across his mood. Until now he hadn't realized how much he'd begun hoping that whole matter came to nothing. If she was Lady Constance and he helped Spence expose her, he doubted she'd take his arm and walk with him, let alone all the other things he'd like her to do.

"I probably haven't used that much paper in my entire life," he said, struggling to decide if he really wanted to know the answer to Spence's charge. On one hand, he did—desperately. Lady Constance's stories were mesmerizing, erotic and uninhibited. Just the thought of Madeline splayed on a chair, naked and aroused, sent a charge of hunger through him.

But on the other hand, he felt suddenly proprietary about the woman on his arm. He wanted to know her secrets, but what right did Spence have to know? Spence only wanted the bounty. He didn't give a damn about what it would do to her. Unlike Douglas, who was beginning to care a great deal more than expected.

"Surely you know how to write a letter?" she asked, interrupting his increasingly alarmed thoughts. "Or perhaps the trouble lies in reading it?"

"Words on a page are easy enough," he said. "I wish I could read you, and know your heart."

She glanced up in surprise; her tone had been teasing, his

almost wistful. "You don't know what you ask for," she murmured.

Douglas's mouth twisted. "I wish I did."

After a few steps in silence, she looked at him again. "Why? That's far more than you wagered for."

He put his hand over hers, still snugly tucked around his elbow. "I'm not here because of a wager."

She faced forward. For the first time in a long time Douglas wished he had a more serious reputation. Why couldn't he have been a smarter fellow, able to notice Madeline on his own? He couldn't stop thinking about her now, and it had nothing to do with Spence's suspicions or his own stung pride. He'd never known another woman like her. In fact, he hoped Spence was wrong. Not because he didn't like to think of Madeline spinning erotic fantasies—by God, he did hope that was true—but because Spence meant to humiliate her in public. He highly doubted she would smile and brush it aside if Spence ruined her name and her livelihood . . . with Douglas's help.

Hell. Bloody, bloody hell.

He banished the thought by taking her to Gunter's. They sat in Berkeley Square under the maple trees and ordered muscadine ices, and Douglas tried to draw her out. This was his specialty; he knew how to pour on the charm. But there was only so much one could expect in such a short time, and all too soon she said she needed to return home. He walked her back to Brunswick Square, feeling at a loss. He was running out of time with her. "Will you go out tonight?" he asked, deciding a blunt question was better than hoping and hinting.

"Still hoping to persuade me to dance?"

He grinned. "Absolutely. But mostly hoping to see you again."

"As soon as tonight?"

*I don't want to leave you now*, he thought, surprising even himself. "Yes."

The direct answer seemed to surprise her, although not unpleasantly. Douglas hoped that meant she was as affected by him as he was by her. He could hardly believe how fascinated he was by everything about her—the sway of her hips, her secretive smile, the way her eyes sparkled when she laughed. It would be cruelly unfair if she felt no attraction to him at all. It would also mean he had completely lost his sense of women. Douglas usually had a finely tuned awareness of a woman's feelings, and right now it was telling him that Madeline not only wanted him, but she was beginning to like him as well.

"Mr. Bennet," she began.

"Douglas," he said. "Please."

She flinched. "Why?"

He leaned toward her. "We're friends now, aren't we?"

"Friends."

"Yes, friends," he repeated firmly, to quell the doubt that edged her tone. "Friends who may take a stroll together, visit the shops together, even go riding together."

"Riding?" Her laugh was a gasp of astonishment. "I do not keep a mount, Mr. Bennet."

"I'll see to that." He felt very virtuous for not suggesting that she could ride him. *Friends*, he reminded himself, not lovers—yet. "Tomorrow morning?"

"Of course not."

"The day after," he countered. "Or the day after that."

They had reached her house. She released his arm and went up the two steps, then turned around. "Are we really friends?"

"I think so." He smiled hopefully. "I would like to be your friend."

"And not something . . . more?"

He went up a step and leaned a little forward. "You know I would like more," he said, gazing steadily into her eyes. "But I also want to be your friend. Someone you can feel at ease with. Someone you can confide in and turn to for help or solace. Someone whom you look forward to seeing every day."

She smiled. "Such lovely sentiments! I see why you're considered the most charming man in London."

"Every word is true."

She studied him thoughtfully, her smile lingering. "I would like to believe it."

"Come riding with me," Douglas said at once. "Driving, if you don't like to ride. Or walking, if you don't like to drive."

After a pause, she nodded. "Perhaps."

"Excellent." He bowed to hide his victorious expression. He looked up in time to see her expression freeze. In an instant her face changed from soft and bright to still and wary. But her eyes weren't on him anymore—she was looking over his shoulder, across the square. "What is it?"

She didn't move except to jerk her eyes back toward him. From a distance she probably looked exactly the same, but up close Douglas could see the color fade from her cheeks. "Nothing. I was startled."

"By whom?" Somehow he knew, he *knew*, what had alarmed her.

The glance she gave him was swift but probing. "A man who was near Gunter's and in Bond Street has just strolled into the square."

He cursed silently. "Someone's following you?"

She hesitated. "It must be a new neighbor. I've seen him several times of late." She edged backward. "Thank you for escorting me, Mr. Bennet."

"Douglas," he said again.

"Good day." Behind her the maid opened the door, as if she'd been waiting, and Madeline ducked into the house. The door closed with a firm thud, and he heard the sound of the bolt being shot.

Douglas has never been known for his quiescent temper; he liked a good brawl and didn't even require a grievous insult to wade cheerfully into one. If someone was following Madeline Wilde—and him—around town, let alone spying on her at home, Douglas would be glad to teach him a lesson.

Deliberately keeping his actions unhurried, he turned around. Under cover of adjusting his hat and checking his watch, he scanned the square. Sure enough, there was a man who seemed to be in no hurry, strolling along the adjacent street. Douglas watched and waited, and was rewarded when the fellow looked directly at him—or rather, at Madeline's house. It was a passing glance, and the man kept walking, right around the corner and out of sight, but one glance was all Douglas needed. He knew who that chap was, and he had a very good guess why he was here.

And he was going to do something about it.

## CHAPTER NINE

He found his quarry late that night in one of the better gaming hells of Whitechapel.

"Looking to take larger lodgings?"

Philip Albright looked puzzled. "No."

Douglas knew Albright lived at The Albany, as did many a bachelor with a modest income. "I hear you've been spending a great deal of time in Brunswick Square. Some handsome houses there." He paused as self-consciousness flickered over the other man's face. "But if you're not after a house to let, it must be a woman, eh?"

Albright shifted his weight. "Perhaps."

Douglas grinned. "Not to worry! I shan't say a word—discretion, you know—provided the woman isn't Madeline Wilde."

"Why would you think that?" blustered Albright, not quite hiding his guilty start.

"Because you've been noticed watching her house. You're giving the lady an attack of nerves. Please stop."

Albright cleared his throat. His eyes roamed the

room, as if searching for an escape. "I don't mean to alarm anyone."

"Standing outside her house at all hours and following her around town would alarm most ladies," Douglas pointed out. "Particularly widowed ladies."

"And she sent you to warn me off?"

"No, she has no idea we're acquainted. I come of my own volition." Douglas leaned closer. "But if William Spence has anything to do with your reasons for frequenting Brunswick Square, you should walk away while you can."

At last Albright met his eyes again. "What does that mean?"

"I know what Spence is up to." He folded his arms. "He made the same offer to me."

"Ah." Albright's expression soured. "And you've stolen a march on me—is that your warning? I saw you with her. I thought that was unusual for you, paying attention to a lady of some respectability. I should have known there was more to it."

Douglas ignored the slight to himself. Yes, he meant to warn Albright to keep far away from her, but he also wanted to know what Spence had told the man, and what Albright might have learned about Madeline. He told himself it was to help her, not to spy on her. His intentions were far more honorable than anything Spence or Albright might plan. "Quite aside from the fact that he's trying to play us against each other—how much did he offer you, by the by?"

"Half of Chesterton's bounty." Now that he'd been found out, Albright seemed to have no inclination to hide anything.

"Only half?" Douglas raised his brows. "When you're putting in all the effort? That's a poor bargain."

Albright frowned. "How much . . . ?"

"Three quarters." He flicked one hand. "Which is still too generous to him, in my opinion . . . *if* the lady turns out to be the one he suspects, which I highly doubt will happen."

Now Albright smirked. "Too generous it might be, but you know Spence. He plays to win. He must have a damned good idea that she's the one, if he went to the trouble of setting us both on it." He peered closer at Douglas. "Tell me true, Bennet—are you asking because you also intend to win, or because you've taken an actual interest in her? If it's the first, then our conversation is over; every man for himself and all that. But if it's the latter . . ."

He had a split second to decide how much he trusted Albright. They'd been friendly since university, frequent opponents in the boxing ring and occasional companions in gaming and general carousing. Albright was a decent companion, not a cheat, and relatively upstanding. He wasn't above making wagers on a lark, but Douglas had never known him to be dishonorable. "The latter," he said in a low voice. "If Spence tries to ruin her, I'll kill him."

Something in the other man's posture eased. "I thought it might be that way. Never seen you look so enthralled by a woman. You didn't even notice when I tipped my hat, did you?"

Douglas blinked. "When?"

"Outside Gunter's." Albright was amused. "*She* saw me."

"I know. It gave her a fright. How long have you been following her?"

"Nearly a month now."

At least a fortnight longer than Douglas had been seeing her. Spence must have grown impatient. "Will you stop?"

Albright nodded. "If you like." He shook his head ruefully. "It seemed long odds, but a thousand quid would have been welcome. I'll tell Spence to bugger off."

"Right. No, wait—don't do that." Douglas thought rapidly. If Albright announced he was out, Spence would probably find someone else to follow Madeline. Albright at least was a gentleman; he might make her nervous but he'd never hurt her or try to terrify her. Some of Spence's other associates weren't as nice in their manners. On no account did Douglas want Spence to send one of them after Madeline. There simply had to be a way to make this rebound on him . . . "Are you willing to turn the tables on him?"

"Sorry?"

"Spence thinks she's Lady Constance. I'm rather sure she's not." Douglas dismissed the fact that he was sure of no such thing, and focused on his main object, which was protecting Madeline—and the best way to help her would be to thwart Spence's plans. He'd never thought himself particularly intelligent, but he had engineered a number of entertaining pranks in his day. Surely this couldn't be that different. And if he played it right, he might come off as rather heroic, which he wouldn't mind at all. "I don't give a damn about the money, but there's no reason you can't make a few pounds off his bloody bargain."

Philip Albright shot him a long, questioning look. For a moment Douglas thought he might laugh or walk away, too distrustful or doubtful, but then Albright said, "All right. Tell me how."

## CHAPTER TEN

For more than two weeks, Mr. Bennet kept up his insistence that they were friends.

He called on her regularly—not every day, but often enough that she began expecting him. He called her Madeline, and wore down her resistance to calling him Douglas by correcting her every time she said "Mr. Bennet." He brought gifts: fresh oranges, a book of poetry, and a beautiful set of swan quill pens. "To fill all those pages of paper," he'd said with a gleam of laughter lurking in his eye. As with all his gifts, she accepted it with thanks. None verged on intimate or romantic, after all, and she'd learned that arguing with him was guaranteed to leave her still in possession of the gift and—despite herself—highly amused. Besides, Constance made a perfectly delicious orange marmalade.

Constance, in fact, found everything about Mr. Bennet perfectly delicious. "Well done, madam," the cheeky maid murmured after one of his calls. "He'll do nicely until Mr. Steele arrives."

"Who is Mr. Steele?" Madeline asked in surprise.

"The butler you ought to hire." Constance tidied the tea tray. "Although his position is in jeopardy now that Mr. Bennet drives you home every night."

That was true, although it left Madeline with conflicting feelings. Douglas attended most of the same events she did, and he invariably insisted on seeing her safely home. It was far more convenient than taking hired hacks, and he always had her laughing by the time they reached her door. He never once asked to come in, or even made an attempt to kiss her. It was all very *friendly*, so much so Madeline was beginning to wonder if she had imagined his earlier, unmistakable attraction to her.

She gave herself a shake. "There's no position to jeopardize."

"Yet," put in Constance.

"Who is this Mr. Steele? You haven't promised someone a position, have you?"

The maid looked wounded. "Never, madam!"

Madeline frowned in suspicion. "Is Mr. Steele a real person, Constance?"

"Not yet." She lifted the tray and got a faraway look in her eyes. "I've pictured him, though; tall enough to reach the top shelves of the larder, and strong enough to carry a lass up the stairs if she should turn her ankle. Fair, I think— fair men are so handsome—with green eyes and a naughty sense of humor. I do admire that in a man, along with broad shoulders and plenty of muscles. His Christian name will be James, or Geoffrey, or something else manly that rolls off a girl's tongue."

"Are you certain it's a butler you picture?" she asked wryly. "He sounds far superior to most butlers."

"I want nothing but the best for you, madam. Mr. Steele should be the top butler in London. But there's no reason he can't be tall, handsome, and strong to boot." The maid grinned and took the tray from the room.

Still smiling in exasperation, Madeline went to the window. The two small boys from next door were chasing a hoop across the grass while their nursemaid watched, and a carriage with two ladies was turning the corner. Brunswick Square was sedate and quiet, with genteel and respectable inhabitants.

And no one else. The man who had once been a regular feature, lingering at the corner or reading a newspaper at the iron fence, was nowhere to be seen. At first she'd been relieved, telling herself she must have been imagining things, but lately she couldn't help wondering if Douglas's frequent visits had anything to do with it.

*Well, good,* she thought. Let it serve some purpose she could defend to Liam. He knew about Douglas's attentions. Twice he'd asked if she wasn't coming to enjoy it, despite her dismissive words. It was harder and harder to deny it, although she maintained that Douglas was no threat. *He's merely my friend,* she imagined telling Liam—and then grimaced as she pictured his reaction to that claim. He probably wouldn't believe it if she told him Douglas was her new guardian, but she thought she could persuade him that she'd been left in peace by everyone else while Douglas was with her.

And yet . . . that was the part that left her conflicted. She should be pleased—elated!—that an amusing, considerate man had decided to befriend her. It was the next best thing to having a brother, who could offer her some protection without requiring her to surrender her freedom. If only she could think of Douglas in a sisterly way.

She realized she was glaring out the window. It was herself she found frustrating, although Douglas was a close second. He must know what he was doing; he knew he was handsome and charming and too entertaining by half. He must be trying to make her mad for him, with this torturous, courteous friendship. Surely if she encouraged him he would sweep her off to bed this very evening and make love to her all night long.

*No.* Madeline shook her head to dislodge the thought. That was not her goal—not having him naked in her arms, with his glib and impertinent tongue doing wicked things to her skin while his hands drove her wild. Not waking up to his lazy grin and thrilling company. Not seeing him cross a crowded ballroom to take her in his arms and demonstrate that she wasn't an icy widow but a woman who had been lonely for far too long . . .

She closed her eyes. She couldn't be falling for him. She'd be the biggest fool in London. He was a gambler, a rogue, a charming rake who was only still interested in her because she hadn't swooned into his arms immediately. The fact that he'd been very decent, even gallant, was only an act. The way he made her laugh was only part of his plot to seduce her.

Surely it was.

After another sleepless night Madeline rose early, dressed, and went out. There was only one person she could turn to for advice on such a subject, only one person who would listen without judgment and never breathe a word about it to anyone. After a brisk walk, she turned into Berwick Street and rapped the knocker at a handsome house of brick.

Her mother was still at breakfast. "Darling," said Adele Dantes, rising from the table with a delighted smile. "How charming to see you."

"You're looking very well, Mama."

"Thank you, darling, you are so kind to an old lady's vanity."

Madeline laughed. "Vain, yes, but not old." She kissed her mother's cheek in greeting.

Adele took her hands and kissed her back, then maintained her grip. She studied Madeline for a moment. "You look preoccupied."

She smiled wryly. "You never miss anything."

"I did not mean to say you look haggard, darling. The shadows are in your eyes, not on your face." Her mother waved her into a seat. "Cecile, bring something for Mrs. Wilde."

As soon as the maid had brought another pot of tea and a place setting for Madeline, Adele dismissed her from the room. "Have you come to talk about it, or to escape it?"

"You know me well, Mama." It was true; she could go weeks without seeing her mother, yet Adele would instantly sense when something bothered her.

Adele gave her a reproachful glance. "I am your mother. I have known your every mood since you were a child."

Madeline stirred a drop of milk into her tea, watching it swirl through the pale amber liquid. Her mother still favored French china, so thin one could see the light shine through it. "I wish it were a simple, childish problem that vexed me now."

"Ah. What is his name?"

She put down the spoon. "Why must it always be a man?"

Adele made a grimace. "It seems to be their nature. What has he done to you? Shall I send Canton to shoot him?"

"No."

"No?" Her mother raised one brow. "He does not deserve to be shot, or you prefer to do it yourself?"

She was saved from a reply to that question when the door opened, and the Duke of Canton himself came in. He was broad and bluff, with thinning hair and an expanding belly. He wasn't a very handsome man, but he was exceedingly good-natured. "Ah, Madeline! Good morning, my dear."

She raised her cheek for his affectionate kiss. "Good morning, Your Grace."

"What a rare treat for me, breakfast with two beautiful women." He winked and turned to give Adele a more passionate kiss. Madeline watched her mother's face shift, becoming more radiant and peaceful. She'd seen that a hundred times before, but for some reason it caught her eye this morning.

The duke circled the room and began lifting lids on the sideboard. "Are there kippers?"

"There are always kippers," said Adele.

He lifted another lid. "Oho! So there are." He glanced at Madeline as he filled a plate. "Have you come to tempt your mama into spending the winter in Hampshire?" The duke's principal seat, Linton Hall, was in Hampshire, a vast estate of bucolic beauty. Every year for as long as Madeline could remember, the duke had been trying to persuade Adele to make an extended visit, and every year he failed. Adele was at home in the city, with its shops and theaters. Every time she gave in to Canton's pleas and went to Hampshire, she found a reason to return to London within weeks, if not days.

"Never say such a thing," replied Adele before Madeline could speak. "How could you tear me away from my only child for the solitude of Linton Hall? I would waste away."

Canton scoffed. "Never! I wouldn't allow it. Come for the Christmas festival, and you'll change your mind, my dear."

Adele waved one hand. "You say that every year, and every year it is so cold and too damp. At least in town one can attend the theater in the rain."

"I'll install a troupe of players just for your amusement. Will you come then?" he cajoled.

She pursed her lips. "I would have to pack every gown I own."

"We'll import a small village of modistes and milliners. They can set up in the great gallery." Canton looked hopefully at Madeline. "And your daughter is always welcome in any home of mine. Surely she would like some country air?"

Madeline couldn't help smiling at him. "Perhaps."

Adele threw up her hands, but Madeline could tell she was trying not to smile, too. "I must reconsider my allies, I see."

"I choose to consider that a prelude to victory," announced the duke. "To Christmastide in Hampshire!" He raised his coffee cup in salute, and they all laughed.

Madeline watched her mother banter with the duke as he ate breakfast and the ladies drank their tea. She'd known Canton her entire life; he had always been there, kind and jovial. When she was a girl, he always had sweets in his pocket for her. As she grew older, he brought her hair ribbons or arranged visits to the menagerie, and when she married he gave her a magnificent pair of diamond earrings. He'd been more like a father to her than her real father, whom she hardly remembered. Henri Dantes had died when she was only six, and her memories of him were limited to a few songs and one time when he took her to fly a kite in the park.

No—that wasn't right. She remembered her father's arguments with her mother. Henri had been a gambler, hardly able to keep a guinea in his fist without staking it in some wager or another. And he'd lost many of them, which had caused the arguments; even as a child she had known that. She remembered hiding behind a chair while her mother screamed at him, a furious stream of French that ended with dishes being thrown. She remembered the night her mother barred the door and refused to admit him when he returned home late at night, drunk and loud. She'd heard him shouting in the street, even with the blankets over her head. After Henri died, Madeline had never heard her mother scream again, and she hardly ever spoke French, either. With his death had come peace, and Canton, and Englishness.

She'd never asked much about it. Her mother never mentioned Henri, but neither did she explain much about the duke. He had been there before Henri died, and he only became a more frequent visitor afterward. He was welcome in Adele's house at all hours, and came and went as if he owned it—which, Madeline suspected, he very likely did. Her mother lived well but discreetly, and any question of money she dismissed as vulgar. Still, Madeline knew what was whispered about her. For years she had heard the rumors, although she had never spoken a word about her family to anyone else. Since childhood her mother had taught her not to acknowledge anything, and she had kept to that. In fact, her ability to keep her own counsel had served her very well.

But watching the two of them this morning made her wonder. Adele had been a widow for nearly twenty years. Canton had never married. There was obviously love and affection between them. There were times when she caught a private glance between them, and she knew there was passion, too. They were rumored to have been lovers for decades, so their marriage would hardly surprise anyone. What kept them apart?

"Tell me about him," said Adele again, when the duke had finished his meal, kissed them both again, and taken himself off, whistling to the dogs who loped at his heels.

Madeline took her time replying. She had come for advice, but now didn't know what to say. How could she describe Douglas? "I was thinking about my father," she said, only realizing when she heard the words that she had wondered about him for a long time.

"He died nineteen years ago, God rest his soul," said her mother evenly. "Who is the man who vexes you?"

She played with her teaspoon. "He's a gambler, like Papa."

"I advise you to drop him at once." Adele's voice had cooled noticeably. "And under no circumstances should you allow him to persuade you he will give it up. If he tries, he is a liar."

She nodded. It was sound advice. All the gossip she heard about Douglas pointed toward, at best, a torrid affair of a few weeks' duration. He was brash and charming and could be very amusing, but he was a rogue. For all she knew, his attention to her could be merely in pursuit of some wager. He'd already admitted wagering on whether he could persuade her to dance with him.

And yet . . . She'd known more than a few unrepentant gamblers in her life, and he wasn't like them. She couldn't picture him in a rage over losing. The rumors of his losses were frequent, but never extreme; in fact, he'd lost several small wagers to her in the last few weeks, and not once had anything darkened his humor. Was it possible for a man to gamble persistently but stay within his means? Had his family covered his losses to spare him the ignominy? Or had he merely been fortunate to have won more than he lost—so far?

"Did Papa always lose?" she asked softly. "I remember the arguments about his losses. Were there also nights he came home flush with winnings?"

Her mother sat in silence for a long time, her gaze fixed on something in the far distance. "Not many. When he won, he took his winnings to the pub, and then . . ." She sighed. "Why must you talk about him?"

"Because I know almost nothing about him." She lifted one hand and let it fall. "All I have are memories of him laughing, and of arguments. As a child I thought he was both wonderful and terrible, and now . . ."

Adele gave her a sideways glance. "He is very like the man you are falling in love with; is that what you are saying?"

"No," said Madeline at once. Her mother's eyebrow rose. "I don't think so."

"You don't think he is like your father, or you are not falling in love with him?"

Neither. She just didn't want to say it out loud. Madeline stared into her tea, wishing she hadn't come. It was horrid to think Douglas was cut from the same cloth as her wastrel father, although the similarities were impossible to deny. That made it all the worse that her mother's second charge was true. She hadn't wanted to like him, but he charmed her. She hadn't wanted to be attracted to him, but she couldn't seem to stop thinking about every little touch of his body against hers, even a mere brush of their hands. She didn't want to fall in love with him, or with anyone, and yet she felt herself slipping a little more each time he made her laugh.

"He must not be entirely like your father, or you would never have given him a second glance," said her mother, breaking into her thoughts. "You certainly never cared for that kind of man before. Arthur was so serious and responsible, so honorable." Adele smiled wryly as Madeline looked up in surprise. "Did you think I didn't notice it? Arthur was unlike your father in every way. He reminded me of Canton, and I approved wholeheartedly of that."

"Mama." Madeline hesitated. "Is Canton . . . Could he possibly be . . . Is he my natural father?"

Adele's spine seemed to wilt a little. She sighed again, and raised her hand to touch two fingers to her lips. "How long have you been waiting to ask that question?"

"Years," she admitted. The first time she'd heard the whispers, she'd wanted them to be true. Canton was kind and amiable and she wanted to be his daughter. Later she had reconsidered, recoiling from the ugly word "bastard." But now she thought it didn't matter. Whether the blood of a reckless gambler flowed in her veins, or the blood of a steady, dependable duke, she was still herself. She believed in luck only so far as she believed that she made her own.

"You are my child," said Adele softly. "*Mine*. Henri never wanted a daughter. Canton is not my husband. You were mine alone, darling, and I was fiercely determined that you would never need a father. But of course you would wonder. I know what people say. The truth is . . ." She hesitated, looking suddenly uncertain. "The truth is that I do not know which of them is your father." She turned her eyes away as Madeline reeled in shock. "I have long felt God would forgive me for infidelity because committing that sin prevented me from a greater one. I did not know how I could live with Henri another day. Canton . . . He surely saved me from murder."

Madeline's mouth was dry. "Did you love him even then?"

"Oh yes." Now Adele's face softened. "Enough that I agreed to anything he proposed. I suspect he paid Henri's debts, just as I know he endured Henri's taunts. He sacrificed his dignity many times for my sake. In turn, I cared nothing for the shocked whispers that I was his mistress. I was very happy to be his mistress. Willingly I closed my eyes to any consequences and went where he led." She put her hand on the table, palm beseechingly open. "But then I had you. I cared for consequences for you when I never did for myself."

"Why didn't you marry him, after—" Madeline stopped before she could say the rest: *after my father died*. Was Henri Dantes her father? She had no idea how to refer to him. "After you were widowed," she finished. "He must have asked."

"It would only have appeared to confirm what everyone said about us," answered her mother. "Neither I nor Canton wanted that, for your sake."

It would have confirmed that her mother had been unfaithful. Madeline knew the duke would have wanted to spare Adele that. "Why did you marry him—Henri—in the first place?"

"Because I was a simpleton." Her mother's expression grew stony. "He was like a hurricane, buffeting me from all sides until I could neither see nor think straight, always cajoling, seducing, never giving me a moment to quiet my senses and think. To be fair, it might not have helped me. I was young and foolish and beside myself with joy at being pursued with such intensity and passion. It turned my head and he knew it."

There was one source of consolation. As flattering as Douglas Bennet's attention had been, Madeline didn't think he'd turned her head. And even though it sometimes felt like a hurricane, most of it had sprung from within herself, when the dawning realization that she liked his attention began warring with her own sense of self-preservation. That had never happened to her before. Her affection for Arthur had dovetailed perfectly with her discretion, and his intentions had been honorable in any event. Their marriage had been safe, secure, peaceful, and content. She feared her fascination with Douglas Bennet would be neither discreet nor honorable, and heaven only knew how it would end.

"This man you are trying not to fall in love with." Adele tapped the table. "Send him away."

She blinked, snapping out of her thoughts. "What?"

"Send him away," her mother repeated. "Set him an impossible task, or a wager he cannot win. If he refuses to go when he loses, you will have your answer. If he keeps his word . . ." She shrugged. "Henri never kept his word. If he had gone away for a week I would have realized how unsuitable he was, and he was determined not to allow that."

"What if he goes and I discover that I don't really wish him gone?" she whispered.

A gentle smile warmed her mother's face. "Then you will get him back, darling. If he is worth your love, he will honor his vow to go, but return at the first word from you. Trust me; I have sent Canton away three times, trying to end it for both our sakes. Every time, I missed him so dreadfully my resolve withered away, and he was on my doorstep within hours."

"What if he doesn't return?"

Adele shrugged. "Then he is not worth your tears. Either way, sending him away will answer your questions."

Madeline supposed it would. If he refused to leave, it would confirm that he had no real respect for her. If he left and didn't return, she would have saved herself humiliation and heartache. But if he behaved honorably, and still wanted to be with her after that . . .

"Thank you, Mama." She rose and kissed her mother's cheek again. "You have been an invaluable help."

Adele clasped her hand, relief softening her face. "What else is a mother for, darling?"

## CHAPTER ELEVEN

Douglas thought his campaign was going beautifully on both fronts.

Albright was proving a first-rate conspirator, throwing himself into the deception with relish. Under the guise of regular boxing matches, they planned what to say and when. Albright expressed growing doubt to Spence that Madeline could be Lady Constance, while Douglas told Spence he was more and more convinced she *was*. He freely padded his accounts with reports of how many times he'd called on her, how welcome he was in her home, and every evening that he left a party or soiree with her on his arm, for all to see, bolstered his credibility. Both he and Albright could see Spence was coming to believe Douglas, and after several days, they agreed it was time for the key play: making another wager with Spence.

"How much should I ask?" Albright asked as they left the boxing saloon after a sparring bout.

"How much do you want?"

Albright considered. "Two hundred would be splendid."

"Good." Douglas nodded. "Not so high he'll be suspicious, not so low to be immaterial."

They both felt Spence deserved to lose some money, but at the moment he had nothing at stake. Without proof of Lady Constance's identity, he would simply sit back and wait. Douglas's goal was to goad Spence into some public declaration, which he could then counterattack and destroy, squashing any suspicion that fell on Madeline. By wagering that Madeline Wilde was *not* Lady Constance, Albright would prod him along; Douglas planned to push him still further by intimating that he saw no reason to split the bounty after all. Keen to win Albright's money and determined not to let Douglas cut him out, Spence would fall right into the trap. Not only would he look like a complete cad, accusing an innocent woman of scandalous behavior, he'd be out two hundred pounds to Albright, without a penny of Chesterton's bounty in recompense.

"I'll approach him tonight." Albright's eyes gleamed with anticipation. "And you?"

"I have plans to take the lady driving tomorrow. I'll be sure to let him know."

His companion laughed. "Well done. I hope you make progress on all counts."

Douglas winked and took his leave. He headed toward home, thinking very pleasurable thoughts about tomorrow.

He had succeeded in getting Madeline to call him by name, and allowing him to do the same. He was welcome in her house, and she seemed happy to see him when they met in society. He made her laugh regularly. Oddly enough, by ceasing all the usual ways of indicating interest in a woman, he seemed to have warmed her feelings toward him. It was a revelation. In his experience women wanted to be charmed and flirted with; they liked the chase as much as he did. But by not pursuing her as hard as he normally would have, Douglas found he knew fascinating things about her.

She hummed when she walked. He thought his ears were deceiving him on one of their strolls through the park, but no—and with a start he recognized a mildly bawdy tune popular in some of the more boisterous taverns. When he caught her eye, incredulous, she merely smiled.

She knew horse racing. He'd never met a woman who cared for anything about a race beyond what gown and hat she might wear, but Madeline knew her horses. She refused to wager on them, but she discussed them with knowledge and interest.

She was left-handed. He discovered this when he called on her one day and saw her bare hands. Traces of ink stained her left thumb and forefinger, and she blithely professed to have been writing letters before he arrived. It made him think—unhappily—of that large quantity of paper again. What was she writing? He could only hope it really was letters and not another erotic recounting of a night of sin.

Even if he could persuade himself it was all fiction, pure works of fancy, he couldn't stand to think of her picturing another man that way, let alone two or three or fifty, even if all the men were as imaginary as the acts. And if she was thinking of *him* as she wrote, that was hardly better; Douglas wanted there to be nothing fictional about their erotic relationship—not that it had begun yet.

With any luck, he'd change that tomorrow.

He had divined that she didn't like crowds, so he chose a quiet spot away from town. With a picnic hamper stowed in the boot and a bright sunny day ahead, he handed her into the carriage. "You've worn good sturdy boots," he said with approval. He'd sent a note with that request earlier.

"You did warn me to." She cocked her head. "Although you didn't explain why."

"That must be a surprise." He sprang up beside her and they were off.

As they drove she tried mightily to guess where he was taking them. He smiled when she said Kensington, laughed when she suggested Greenwich, but he almost drove off the road when she asked, almost slyly, "Are you stealing me away to Gretna Green?"

"What? No," he protested, fighting to control the horse. Like the carriage, it was hired for the day, and he had yet to get a feel for the animal or vehicle. His sudden tightening of the reins had nothing to do with her implication.

"No, I see not." Her eyes shone as she laughed at him. "The mere suggestion of elopement almost cost us both our lives."

"Nothing like that." The horse finally settled back into a steady trot, with an occasional toss of his head. Douglas told himself the sudden jolt of danger had caused his heart to pound, not the idea of carrying Madeline away to Gretna Green, just the two of them, sharing every moment of every day . . . and night . . . on the long road north. That would be a very dashing way to prove his interest was honorable— although it would leave him married. To her.

He glanced at her from the corner of his eye. She still

wore a pleased smile, as if she'd bested him in some way. Did she mention Gretna Green because she had been thinking of marriage? To him?

"Do gentlemen regularly attempt to carry you off to Gretna?" he asked, unsettled by the whole line of thought.

"No, this would be my first time." She tipped her head in that way she had, so that she was looking up at him around her bonnet brim. "I suppose it would be your first as well."

"It would." He cleared his throat. "I daresay this carriage isn't adequate to the journey." It was an open curricle, comfortable for a short drive but no more.

"Decidedly not."

"It would be presumptuous to set off for Gretna without being certain the lady wished to be married."

"Very."

"And yet," he said slowly, "you didn't leap from the carriage at the thought." He glanced at her just as she looked at him. Their eyes met and for a moment he wondered if maybe—

She faced forward again and laughed lightly. "Why should I? People go to Gretna to be married. I feel entirely safe from marriage with you."

He frowned. Marriage wasn't on his mind, and yet . . . "Now why would that be? Neither of us is already married. It's certainly *possible*."

"But not plausible." Madeline's brows went up and her lips curved, as if she was about to hear a juicy bit of gossip. "Or perhaps I am mistaken. Have you decided to wed?"

"No," Douglas said before he could stop himself. He hadn't, not at all, but the idea that she had completely dismissed him that way rankled. He was an eligible match, damn it. If he did want to wed, he could find a willing bride within days. Madeline had no right to feel *safe* around him, not when he wanted her with an almost unbearable hunger. Not for marriage, true, but she should at least be aware of the possibility.

"And that's why I'm not worried." She touched his hand. "We both know you're not a marrying man."

He was still brooding over that as he turned off the road and brought the carriage to a halt. With some effort he shook off those thoughts—what a wretched thing to spoil his carefully planned excursion, marriage—and summoned a smile. "Are you ready to work?"

She looked around in bemusement. The carriage sat at the edge of an orchard, and a servant was coming toward them with baskets. "At what?"

"Cherry picking. They're just coming into season, and we have the trees to ourselves for the day."

Incredulous delight dawned on her face. "Cherries?"

"My favorite." He grinned, feeling an unexpected burst of relief that she was pleased. He jumped down and held out his hand to help her out of the curricle. "I expect to take home a full pail, so you'll have to pick your own if you want to do the same."

"So unchivalrous!" But she took the pail the servant handed her and headed toward the grove with him.

For an hour they picked cherries. Douglas set the ladders against the trees, but she waved aside his offer of assistance. She caught him stealing an appreciative glance at her ankles as she climbed, and she pelted him with cherries until he retreated to another tree.

"Why cherries?" she asked when they had filled their baskets and come down from the ladders to enjoy the picnic lunch.

"Stealing fruit from the orchards was one of my sins as a lad." He popped one into his mouth. "Cherries are my favorite."

"A thief!" She laughed.

"Guilty. But worth every bit of penance. Tell me you don't agree." He picked out a cherry so ripe it was nearly black and held it in front of her lips.

"I've eaten so many, my mouth will be scarlet forever." She pursed her lips into a pout to illustrate.

Douglas's eyes riveted on her mouth. The fruit dropped from his fingers and gently he touched one fingertip to that pout. "Beautiful," he murmured. She didn't move, seemingly as fascinated as he was. Her expression subtly altered, softening until she almost looked surprised. Slowly he leaned toward her, braced to stop at any sign from her. Instead her face tipped up toward him, and her eyes fluttered closed a moment before he kissed her.

He felt like a boy again, hardly able to breathe for the excitement coursing through him. His heart beat against his ribs like a mallet. Her mouth was soft under his, as sweet as the cherries. When her lips parted under his, a shudder ran through him. She turned into his arms, her hands landing on his arms. He cupped her jaw and deepened the kiss until he felt drunk on the taste of cherries and her.

With a soft moan, she leaned into him. Her arms circled his neck and she didn't protest when he pulled her into his lap—instead she parted her knees and straddled him, pressing against him as she kissed him back with enough passion to make him lose his mind. Blindly he undid the buttons of her pelisse, baring her skin to his hungry eyes.

"Madeline," he gasped, raining kisses down her throat. "My God. I can't think of anything but you."

Her spine arched as he tugged off her pelisse. "As a friend?"

He groaned. Her skin was as tempting as fresh cream. "That and more. Let me make love to you."

She went very still. "What do you mean?"

Douglas traced his fingertip along her collarbone. "Let me show you."

She shivered. "The way you show tavern maids and ballet dancers?"

His finger stopped.

"Let me guess. They are coy and coquettish. They simper and giggle. Then they take you into their beds, or let you carry them off to yours, and let you have your way." She shook her head, even though she still sat astride him, breathless and seductively mussed. "Girls like that know how delicate a man's dignity is. I can hear how they cry out, moaning and screaming as you bend them over or bid them straddle you on a chair."

"What have you got against chairs?" he asked in a low voice.

Her eyelashes fluttered, the only sign his words affected her. "Nothing. But that is not making love. That is tupping."

Douglas ran his hand down her back, imagining her bare skin. "Does it matter what you call it if both people find it highly satisfying?"

"So they tell you—but they're well paid to do so, aren't they?"

He smiled and lowered his lips to her bosom again. "Money has nothing to do with it."

She drew back. "Are you sure of that?"

"Yes," he said at once.

This time she shrugged. "Then try it. The next time you have one on your knee, eager for a romp in bed, tell her you have no coin. Tell her you are destitute, and see how eagerly she leads you up the stairs for a tumble."

Douglas pulled a face, half amused, half annoyed at her insistence. "I'd rather have you show me what you think making love should be."

She lifted his chin. His gaze snagged on her lips, soft and red and parted in invitation. "Try it."

He didn't really want to think of a buxom barmaid on his knee right now, not when he was consumed by thoughts of Madeline. Just the thought of leaning forward and kissing her until she gave up this nonsense about the difference between tupping and making love was driving him wild. "You seem very sure of it," he said, trying to keep his mind focused on the conversation. "What would you wager on it?"

He knew as soon as he said it that it had been a bad idea. Hadn't he lost every wager with her so far? But it was too late now, and maybe his luck was about to turn. It was certainly due. He didn't like to think that it would be a lost wager that got her into his bed, but at the moment, he was reckless enough to chance anything.

Her shoulders straightened and her lips compressed. He

caught a flash of gold in her eyes. She scrambled off his lap and took a long look at him, from his boots to the top of his head. Her unashamed and unhurried study sent the blood roaring through his veins. God, he wanted this woman, and he'd wager his last possession to get her. "If I'm right and she turns you aside, you won't speak to me again, or call on me, or trouble me in any way."

Douglas recoiled. He didn't want to agree to that. "Why that?"

"Why not that? If you're certain you're right, what does it matter what I might win? You have nothing to lose."

He didn't like it. He didn't wager what he couldn't bear to lose. "You'd have to balance that with something very tempting indeed."

"Hmm." She tilted her head. "If you win . . . Let me think, what would tempt you? If you win . . ." She paused for a long moment. Douglas's imagination ran wild, picturing all the things he'd like to win from her. "If you win, I will publicly own authorship of my writing."

## Chapter Twelve

Douglas stared. How the devil—? Curse it all, giving her those quills had been a mistake. He'd tried so hard to hide his curiosity about that large order of paper, and had obviously failed. "What?" He tried to recover. "What writing?"

Her glance was almost reproachful. "Asking if I intend to write a novel or publish a newspaper. You suspect me of something. That's what you wagered on the night you first spoke to me, isn't it? Someone has dared you to discover my secret."

"No," he said indignantly. "It was for a dance." The wager she mentioned hadn't happened until after he spoke to her, therefore what she said wasn't exactly true.

She didn't look persuaded. "No?"

He could feel his face getting hotter, which only made him act more affronted. "I don't know what you're talking about."

"We aren't true friends if you would lie to me so easily." She rose and started to walk away.

There was a battle within Douglas's breast, harsh and swift. He vaulted to his feet. "If that's what you wish to stake, so be it. But it's not something I care to win."

"Perhaps you won't." Her face was averted, but her body was as taut as his.

Now he really didn't want to make this wager. Lose, and he'd have to bow out of her life forever. Win, and his ugly, ill-considered bargain with Spence would come out. Spence was too much of a scoundrel not to tell of collecting the bounty, and if he sensed Douglas no longer wanted any part of it—and Douglas didn't think he'd be able to hide that—Spence would take great delight in "sharing" the credit for solving the mystery. Then Madeline would see him for what he was, or at least what he had been: an idle gambler who wagered without thought or care for the subject of his bets.

Damn it. Either way, he was going to lose her.

"Never mind a wager," he said abruptly. "I shouldn't have suggested one."

"No?" Still she didn't look at him. "You're afraid you'll lose."

And just as afraid he might win. "You said you don't wager. I was wrong to press the issue."

"But that's your usual way of settling matters, isn't it? So we shall wager, as you wished. Am I not to be treated with the same honor and respect you would accord other gentlemen wishing to test each other?"

There had to be a flaw in her argument, but Douglas didn't see it. He was doomed if he took it, but if he didn't she might begin to wonder why he wanted to back out only after hearing her stake. He cursed himself for not being more temperate and canny. "I hardly think of you in the same way I regard other gents wishing to wager," he said stiffly, "but if you insist, we have an agreement."

All brightness and humor of the outing fled. It was a quiet and uncomfortable drive back to town. He racked his brain for any way out. It had seemed such a lark: Expose the infamous Lady Constance, and get to sample her charms in person. Somewhere along the way, though, the nebulous figure of Constance had diverged from the very real, very intriguing Madeline. He cared nothing for the feelings of Constance, who was surely tempting fate by writing as she did, but for Madeline . . . For Madeline, he was coming to care a great deal. And if they turned out to be one and the same . . . he didn't know what he'd do.

In Brunswick Square she stepped down without waiting for his assistance. "Thank you for the cherries," she said quietly. "It was a lovely outing."

Until the end. He scrambled after her, not even bothering to tie up the horse. "I only meant to bring you pleasure," he said, trying one last time to extricate himself. "As one friend to another. I wish . . ."

She regarded him steadily. "You wish to be more than friends."

He did. He thought about kissing her every time she opened her mouth. He thought about holding her every time his hand touched hers. "I do," he said, undaunted by how rough and pleading his voice sounded. Perhaps it would spur her to relent, at least on that wager. He knew she was attracted to him. Hadn't he proved himself honorable and decent? Hadn't he won any small part of her affections? It would be crippling if she really cared nothing for him. "Every day I scheme for some excuse to call on you. I look forward to tedious balls and soirees because I know you'll be there. You enchant me, Madeline, and while I want to be your friend . . . Yes, I also want much more."

For a moment it seemed to have worked. Her lips parted and her eyes widened with wonder. He eased a few inches closer and dared to run his fingertips over the back of her hand, still clutched around the basket handle. "Will you give me a chance? Forget the wager. Don't say you want to turn me away forever . . ."

She flinched and stepped backward, away from his touch. "Are you crying off?"

Douglas curled his hand into a fist. "Yes. Unless you insist upon it."

"I do," she murmured. "We shall see what Fate decides. Good-bye, Mr. Bennet."

He was left standing on the step, bereft, as she went inside without another word. Slowly he turned back to the curricle, fortunately still there. The horse could have trotted off to Islington and he wouldn't have noticed.

Damn it. How could he avoid losing that wager? Could he just never put it to the test? She had all but admitted she was Lady Constance, and she must know what it would mean to publicly confess it. Why on earth had she staked that?

Because she wanted him out of her life forever. *You won't speak to me again*, she'd said.

Douglas was caught off guard by how hard that hit him. Hadn't she been happy with him today? Perhaps she didn't think him worthy of marriage, but surely at least as a friend . . . ? Not that he wanted to be only her friend. More than ever he yearned to be free to take her hand, to see her eyes light up when he came into the room, to share a private joke with her and know that he had made her laugh. Even if he never had the pleasure of kissing her, holding her, making love to her, he would miss that impish delight in her face when he said something amusing.

He would miss . . . her.

## CHAPTER THIRTEEN

M adeline suffered alternating bouts of doubt, regret, and misery all day.

Douglas's plea had nearly wrecked her resolve. *He does care*, whispered a little voice inside her head. *Are you mad to turn away such a man?* Her conscience tried to argue: *Everything is a wager to him, and as soon as he wins you over he'll lose interest.* She began to regret following her mother's counsel to send him away. Instead of making her feel better, Douglas's reluctance to take the unwinnable wager had only torn at her heart. Leaning against her door with a basket of cherries clasped in her arms, listening to the faint rattle of wheels as he drove away, Madeline tried to quell the sinking feeling that she'd made a mistake.

*This is an important test*, she told herself. It had sounded much easier and definitive when her mother had described it, but she could endure it—in fact she must—because she desperately needed to know the truth of Douglas's intentions. Were all his signs of friendship solely to seduce her, or had he actually come to care for her? *Give me a chance*, he'd begged.

He even tried to cry off from the wager, undermining his roguish reputation.

"Stop it," she hissed. Her hands were shaking, she was gripping the basket handle so hard. He tried to cry off because he didn't want to give her heart and mind time to calm down and reach the sensible conclusion that he was no good for her. Mama was right. As long as he kept seeking her out at balls and driving her home and walking with her on tedious errands around London and taking her on beautiful picnics to orchards, she would remain in this feverish state of attraction and longing . . . and hope. Hope that she would be the one who inspired him to change his ways. Hope that his attentions weren't all a ploy to seduce her. Hope that she wasn't an idiot to feel as giddy as a girl in the first throes of love every time he caught her eye and grinned.

"You are not in love with him," she whispered, still scolding herself furiously. She was a sane, sensible woman who would not be so foolish as to lose her head—or her heart—over any man of Douglas's reputation. He was a rogue, a gambler, a notorious rake who pursued women on whims and discarded them just as capriciously. Her mother would be horrified to see her falling for such a man.

Of course Mama had also admitted her resolve to leave Canton never lasted once he went away. Could Douglas be the same as Canton? He hadn't even been gone an hour and already Madeline yearned to run through the streets until she found him and called off the wager.

"Madam?"

At the sound of Constance's uncertain query, Madeline gave a shriek and nearly dropped the cherries. She clapped one hand to her throat, where her heart seemed to have jumped. "Yes?"

Her maid drew back a step. "A note for you from Mr. MacGregor. It arrived while you were out."

"Oh." Madeline stared at the paper Constance offered. "Yes. Thank you." Belatedly she remembered she had an appointment with Liam later today. She handed Constance the basket and read the note. Liam only wanted to delay their appointment half an hour, which was fine with her. It would probably take that long for her heart to beat normally again.

"Is aught wrong?" asked Constance, still looking at her askance.

"Of course not. What makes you ask that?"

"The way you leapt like Mr. Nash at the sight of water when I spoke." Constance examined the cherries. "Mr. Bennet, I suppose. I've a mind to send George to thrash him."

"George?" Madeline blinked in confusion.

"I've been thinking a footman might be a sight more useful than a driver or a butler. He'd be in the house most of the time, which would be handy even when there isn't a gent in need of thrashing—"

Madeline gave her a jaundiced look. "Bored of Mr. Steele already?"

The maid shrugged. "Footmen's wages are lower than butler's. I thought the odds of George might be greater. He needn't be tall, just strong. I imagine he'll have dark eyes and long hair, down to his shoulders—just right for a girl to run her fingers through . . ."

"Who said Mr. Bennet needed thrashing?" Madeline ignored the speculation about nonexistent footmen and took off her pelisse. She would have to change before her appointment with Liam; there were grass stains on her skirt and spots of cherry juice on the bodice where Douglas had kissed her—

"You went out with him smiling and humming, and come home looking as though he ripped out your heart and took it with him." Constance glanced at her reproachfully. "It's not my place—"

"No, it isn't."

"—but I'd say he did something wrong."

Madeline gripped the newel post for strength. What had he done wrong? He'd made her want to fall in love with him. "It's not your place," she told the maid quietly but firmly. "I have a feeling Mr. Bennet shan't be around much longer for you to worry about."

"Shall you advertise for George, then?" Constance called after her as she hurried up the stairs. "Or Mr. Steele?"

"No!"

Madeline tried not to think about Douglas after that. She dashed off a note to her mother relating what had happened, hoping Mama would reassure her she had done the right thing. She sent Constance to deliver it, then forced herself to finish her piece for Liam. Normally she took pride and pleasure in her writing, but not today. She wondered how Douglas had come to suspect her of writing for the *Intelligencer*. Liam was the only person who knew for certain. Constance probably knew, although Madeline had never told her directly. But Douglas looked so guilty when she said she would publicly own her writing. He must have made a wager about it; perhaps that was the only reason he had ever paid her attention.

Mr. Nash jumped onto the desk and walked across the

page. Madeline started to scold him, but gave up. She stroked his back. "Tell me I did well," she murmured to the cat. He sat right on top of her paper and gazed at her, purring loudly. With a reluctant smile she scooped him into her arms and buried her face in his black and white fur. "I still wish I hadn't done it."

At four she went to Wharton's Bank, a short walk away. Liam was already there, sprawled in the chair with one foot on the fender. "I hope you weren't waiting long," she told him, taking the opposite chair and laying her packet on the table between them.

"No." Liam studied her. "When we began this . . . partnership, how long did you expect it to last?"

She lifted one shoulder. "As long as it was profitable. Perhaps a month, perhaps years."

"It's been nearly a year. Are you still pleased with the arrangement?"

A fortnight ago she would have laughed at him for asking. Today she could only manage an indifferent "Yes."

Liam's sharp eyes were relentless. "You haven't grown tired of keeping it secret? Of moving among the cream of society and reporting their indiscretions?"

Madeline sighed. "If you want to know something, please ask."

"Will you give me warning before you marry Douglas Bennet? The *Intelligencer* really should have that news first."

She started. "Marry—? Where on earth did you get that idea?"

"One of the most eligible bachelors of the *ton*, who previously avoided any ball unless the card room rivaled a gaming hell, now makes his way directly to your side and spends every evening there. He drives you home. He squires you around town." He raised his brows. "What idea did you think that would give?"

She clenched her hands together in her lap. "He's not a marrying man."

Liam laughed. "So says every man until he meets the woman who undoes him!"

Longing shivered through her. "Nevertheless, it's not marriage on his mind. And I've taken steps to get rid of him." It gave her a physical pain in her chest to say those words.

"You told me that weeks ago. Either you didn't mean it or you underestimate his interest."

"He suspects I write for you," she said abruptly. "He may mean to expose me." If she didn't distract him, Liam would soon pry out of her that his charge was true on both counts: She didn't want to drive Douglas away, and part of her desperately hoped his interest was even greater than she knew.

Liam shot out of his chair. "How the hell—?"

"I don't know." She pressed one hand to her temple. "So you may believe me when I tell you I'm trying to turn him away."

He went down on one knee beside her. "Madeline. I can have someone warn him off. I told you to let me deal with this." She lowered her hand. He took a look at her expression and his shoulders sagged. "Tell me you're not in love with him."

She summoned a bittersweet laugh. Of course Liam would notice. "I'm trying to fight it off."

He hung his head and sighed. "And failing miserably, I

gather. Well." He laid his hand over hers. "I should have him tied up and thrown into the Thames."

"Don't be ridiculous." She got to her feet and smoothed down her pelisse. "I don't know if he would expose me, but it means I must tread carefully. Perhaps it's best if that's the last piece for a while." She nodded at the sealed packet on the table.

"Yes." He too rose, and tucked the report into his pocket. "My mother will be desolated if I lose you permanently."

"It seems to me she hears plenty of gossip on her own," she replied tartly.

Liam winked. "It's never enough. For my sake, persuade Bennet not to spoil things."

She didn't deign to reply to that. Liam's opinion was important to her, but the *Intelligencer* consumed him. Of course he would prefer that she remain as she was, aloof and remote and free to spend her time gathering gossip for his newspaper. That didn't mean his advice was wrong, but she found herself discounting it as she walked home. Liam was her friend, not her father, and how did he know what she really wanted? Not even she knew that.

The note waiting at home from her mother only reinforced her discontent. Mama consoled her on the melancholy she must be feeling but assured her it would lead to greater happiness. "Only when you know his true desires can you be sure of your own path," Mama wrote. Madeline sighed as she read that. How easy for Mama to say that, with steady, reliable Canton devoted to her. She must have known he would come back to her no matter how many times she sent him away. If only Madeline could know the same about Douglas . . .

That was when she admitted defeat. She wanted him to come back. What if, when he lost—and she was absolutely sure he would—he went away, as she asked . . . and then had no interest in returning? She had outsmarted herself, devising a plan to rid herself of a man who had stolen her heart.

If only she had realized it in time.

CHAPTER FOURTEEN

Douglas eyed the pub grimly. It was one of his favorites, where the girls were friendly and the ale was strong, and tonight it looked like the gatehouse to hell.

It seemed days had passed instead of hours since he'd made that wretched wager with Madeline. He'd spent most of those hours trying to think of a way around it. If he never went back to a tavern he could simply say it was still an open question, that no one had lost and no one had won. He could continue seeing her . . . and wondering all the while why she'd wanted to win his absence. Was she only tolerating him? Had he so completely lost his touch with women that he'd misread every sigh and smile and even that kiss, the kiss that promised to torment him for the rest of his life? Finally, in some despair, he decided to get it over with.

As usual, he barely found a chair before he had company. Amy, a jolly girl with dark red hair, hurried over when she saw him. "Mr. Bennet! You've not been here in ages! Haven't you missed me?"

"I'm missing you right this moment, Ames," called a

fellow seated at the next table over. "Come over and make me feel welcome, won't you?"

She made a face and turned her shoulder to the man as his companions bellowed with laughter. "Never mind them," she said to Douglas, sliding onto his knee. "A pack of scoundrels."

His stomach clenched. *Scoundrels are dishonest at heart.* Was he any better? "Amy."

She settled comfortably in his lap, her arm around his neck. "Aye, love? Shall we go upstairs and have a more private conversation?"

He turned his head aside when she tugged playfully at his hair, and dodged her attempt to kiss him. "Perhaps in a moment. What is it to you, when we go upstairs?"

"A bloody good time!" She giggled. Her hand was inside his waistcoat, easing down his belly.

Douglas barely felt it, which was odd. Usually he liked a bold wench, and Amy was as bold as they came. Anything he suggested, she was keen to try. He'd had some remarkable evenings with her. And yet . . . Madeline's words festered in his mind. What a stupid wager this was. He couldn't bear to lose, and he didn't want to win. He shifted in his seat, trapping Amy's hand inside his waistcoat. "You're fond of me, aren't you?"

She stared at him, then smiled—coyly, damn it. "You know I am! A big brawny fellow like you, and so handsome, too." She ran her fingers through his hair.

"How fond?" he persisted, beginning to feel like an idiot. At this very moment he could see three other barmaids, all flirting openly with other patrons. Of course they must be thinking of what those men might bestow upon them after a night of pleasure. Douglas was always generous, too, but he told himself that was due to the rare sort of contentment that filled a man after making love. So Madeline was partly right. He still thought women were glad to see him aside from his money.

"Mmm, have you got something especially naughty in mind tonight?" She wriggled her hand free of his waistcoat and plucked at his cravat. "What is it?"

"It . . ." His voice died. He didn't want to take Amy upstairs at all. Not when all he could think about was Madeline's brown eyes, teasing him, scorning him, glowing golden in delight with him. "It's just that I haven't got any more funds."

Amy's fingers paused in their wandering. "None at all?"

"No," he said. "My father cut me off. I won't have a farthing for months, so I can't give you anything as I did before." Amy stared at him, her blue eyes shadowed. "Will you still go upstairs with me?"

She bit her lip and glanced over her shoulder. "Well . . ."

"Does that mean no?"

She looked torn. "You're awfully sweet, Mr. Bennet, truly you are. More than most men! But it's late, and if I go upstairs with you . . ."

"You'd be wasting your time because I haven't got money?" he finished when she fell silent.

"Not wasting," she said quickly. "Only . . . I got duties here! I'll lose my place if I don't serve and clean."

That had never bothered her before, when she'd gone upstairs without a backward glance at the taproom. Douglas let her slide off his lap. "I understand."

Relief brightened her face. "I knew you would! But if your

fortunes change . . . you know where to find me." She grabbed an empty mug from the next table and headed toward the bar, her russet curls bobbing in her haste.

Douglas exhaled slowly. Thank God. He felt no dismay, no regret over the loss of Amy's company, not even a tingle of indignation that he'd been utterly, spectacularly wrong. For a moment all he felt was an overpowering sense of relief that his offer to take her upstairs hadn't been accepted.

But his reward would be the permanent loss of Madeline's company. What a colossal mistake. The only good thing was that Madeline wouldn't be obliged to ruin herself. He wasn't sure she was being truthful about her stories; he noticed she'd said she would claim authorship, not confess that she was the author. But now she wouldn't have to do that, because she'd won.

He pushed back his chair and rose, feeling a little numb. The cool night air hit him in the face as he shoved open the pub's door. For several minutes he walked, not seeing where he went. He'd lost, and honor demanded he acknowledge it and pay his forfeit. He kicked a loose cobble in frustration. Why had he ever mentioned wagering to her?

Because he was an idiot to risk what he couldn't bear to lose. If only he'd realized it in time.

He turned into Gower Street, not knowing what he would do when he got to her house. The half-mile walk was over in a blink and he found himself on her step, looking up at her windows. A light shone in the upstairs one. He imagined it was her bedroom. He pictured her in a lacy night rail, her unbound hair falling like silk around her shoulders, her eyes soft with welcome at his arrival . . .

And now it would never happen. His stupid penchant for wagers had finally ruined him.

"Bloody hell," he muttered, squeezing his eyes shut. Grimly he straightened his shoulders and rapped the knocker. It was late and the sound echoed up and down the street. It was several minutes before he heard the bolt being drawn back, and the door opened.

"Douglas . . ." She held up a lamp, shedding a golden glow over her face. He stared in longing. Her night rail wasn't silk and lace, but sturdy cotton buttoned all the way up—and somehow it was the most seductive thing he'd ever seen. Her hair did fall over her shoulders, as dark as honey in the light of her lamp.

But her eyes were wide with surprise, not soft with welcome, and she held the door open only a few inches, as if afraid he would leap on her. He took a deep breath. "I came to say you've won our wager."

She blinked.

"You were entirely right that my charms spring chiefly from my purse," he went on, like a penitent scourging himself. "If I were a lamplighter, I daresay I'd not know what it was like to kiss a woman, let alone bed one. You have torn the veil of delusion from my eyes, and I humbly acknowledge your victory." His jaw clenched against the next words, but he forced himself onward. "I suppose then this is also our farewell, since I wagered my eternal absence from your life. I cannot swear we'll never cross paths at some *ton* party, but you have my word I won't approach you or speak to you." He hesitated, hoping, but she just stared at him in openmouthed astonishment. Douglas bowed stiffly. "Good-bye, Madeline. I wish you a very happy life."

# Chapter Fifteen

Madeline thought she must have whacked herself on the head and not realized it. Her first reaction had been a blinding surge of happiness; he had come to tell her the wager was immaterial because he loved her. Instead . . . he was conceding. And leaving. "What did you do?"

"What you told me to do. I sat a wench on my knee and asked if she would tumble me even if there wasn't a ha'penny in it for her."

*Fool girl.* The thought slipped through her mind before she could stop it. "I'm sorry it cost you an evening's pleasure."

His dark gaze dropped to her mouth. He was subdued tonight, all his charm and good humor banished. "It didn't."

She flushed. Of course not. "Imagine my relief."

"You were right about all of it. I didn't even want to tumble her. I realized it as soon as she sat on my knee and put her arms around my neck, and all I could do was wish she was someone else." He put out his hands in a gesture of surrender. "But that person will never put her arms around my neck, because she doesn't want to see me ever again." Without another word he turned and walked away, every strike of his boot heel making her flinch as he disappeared from her life.

She clutched her lamp. She didn't want him to go. That stupid wager. Yes, she'd meant it when she threw out the challenge, and at the time it had seemed like the ultimate escape. If he no longer called on her or sought her out, she wouldn't have to think about her growing feelings for him. She wouldn't have to admit how much she thought of him. How much he made her laugh. How tempted she was to throw herself at him and let him make love to her every night for the rest of her life.

His steps slowed. In the circle of light from a streetlamp, he stopped. Madeline's heart leapt. Wordlessly she gripped the doorknob as he turned around and met her gaze. For a long moment they both stood there, and then he started back toward her.

"I can feel you watching me," he said.

She wet her lips. "Don't be ridiculous. No one can feel that."

"Right. You know exactly what I feel and what I think and what I know." He reached the few steps to her door.

"I never said that."

He stopped in front of her and pushed the door open all the way. "Then don't think it, either, at least for the next few minutes." And with that, he tipped up her chin and kissed her.

His kiss was soft and gentle, seductive. His lips were warm, and when he teased the corner of her mouth with his tongue, she gave in with a gasp of pent-up joy. His kiss was hungry and thorough, as if he thought he'd only have this taste and meant to savor every moment of it.

She had sent him away once, but wouldn't make the same mistake again. She slid her arm around his neck and pressed herself against him, barely keeping a grip on the lamp she still held.

He broke the kiss. His arms tightened around her waist and held her to him, dragged up on her toes. He rested his forehead against hers. His shoulders heaved with every ragged breath.

"I'm sorry," he whispered, his words warm against her lips. "I'm sorry I was an ass when we first met. I'm sorry I upset you so much that you made that wager to get rid of me. And I'm desperately sorry this is all I'll have to remember you by, because I think I've lost my heart to you, Madeline." His mouth met hers before she could say a word, another long, mesmerizing kiss that made her knees go soft and her skin grow hot.

She didn't want to get rid of him. She needed him. He infuriated her and challenged her and made her laugh at the worst moments. She wanted to burrow into his arms and make him wild for her, so wild he forgot every other woman he'd ever held—that would only be fair, since she doubted any other man could ever dominate her thoughts and feelings the way he did.

Her mother's advice had been perfect. She'd sent him away, and he had admitted he was wrong, admitted he had lost, and made his farewell. He had behaved honorably. "Don't," she breathed when he lifted his head again. *Don't stop. Don't go. Don't leave me.*

"Don't what?"

She touched his lip. "Don't leave."

He was motionless for a moment. "If I stay, it won't be merely for tonight. I want to come back tomorrow. I want to dance with you at every ball in London, and I want to bring you home afterward and take you to bed for the rest of the night. Don't ask me to stay if you don't want all that, too."

Madeline nodded. It was all she could manage. His words sparked such a craving within her, she could barely breathe. Without another word, he took the lamp from her paralyzed fingers and set it aside. He lifted her off her toes and carried her back inside the house. He never let go of her as he closed the door and shot the bolt.

"Which way?" He caught her around the knees and swung her effortlessly into his arms.

"The door on the left at the top of the stairs." She put her arms around his neck, thrilling at the feel of his muscles flexing as he carried her. She pressed her lips against his jaw, and was rewarded with a low growl of approval. With one flick of her hand, she sent his hat tumbling down the stairs so she could comb her fingers through his hair.

He walked through her house as if he'd been there a hundred times, shouldering open her sitting room door and shoving it closed with one foot. He turned his head to kiss her again as he let her feet back down to the floor. Between hungry kisses, they worked at stripping Douglas. Layer by layer his clothing fell to the floor until he yanked his shirt over his head, baring his very splendid chest to her view. Madeline gasped, and he gave her a little push away.

"Take it off," he commanded in a silky whisper.

Her face heated, but not with embarrassment. Without a word she unbuttoned her night rail and let it fall. The rush of air on her skin was cool, but she felt feverishly hot. Douglas's hands fisted; his stomach flexed. His eyes seemed to burn as his gaze moved over her.

"Do you need me to be gentle?" His voice had become rough. "Should I try to go slowly?"

"Please don't," she managed to say before he caught her to him and sealed his mouth to hers in a kiss that made the room spin. She plowed her hands into his hair, shamelessly pressing against his body. His hands slipped around her bottom and he lifted her until she curled her legs around his waist. He moaned and flexed his spine, and Madeline's lungs seized. His unfastened trousers hung around his hips but she could feel him, hard and big, and if not for the trousers, he would be inside her already. No, she did not need him to be gentle or slow.

"Thank God. I'm all out of patience at the moment." He carried her the few steps across the room to the chaise and laid her on her back before him. He kicked off his trousers and went down on his knee between her legs. "You've driven me half mad today."

She laughed, feeling a little mad herself. Her back arched as his hands moved over her. His fingernails scraped down her ribs and she twisted; he cupped her breast and she almost stopped breathing. He loomed over her and caught her nipple between his teeth, bringing her to the brink of climax. When he bent his head and began tracing his way down her belly with his tongue, she plowed her fingers into his hair and yanked.

"Just one taste," he muttered, catching her hands and holding them away.

"Douglas," she moaned in longing, and then his mouth settled between her thighs. She writhed, but his grip on her hands was like iron, his shoulders pinned her legs, and she was utterly defenseless against the overwhelming pleasure he lavished on her.

He lurched upright. "Sweeter than cherries," he rasped. "And so ready . . ."

"Yes." Madeline was almost weeping. "*Yes.*"

His grin flashed, strained and victorious. "As you command, love." And he thrust deep.

Madeline gave a little cry. Douglas shuddered, his fingers digging into her hips. Both were too frenzied for tenderness. It was a rough, primal coupling that shook the chaise and ended in a few moments, leaving both of them spent and breathing raggedly.

"I knew you'd be wild in bed." He pressed a lingering kiss to her shoulder.

"I blame you," she said faintly.

His grin was fierce. "Good." His head dipped, and he ran his tongue around her straining nipple. "I want to drive you wild."

"Let me touch you." She reached for him, and this time he let her caress his face.

"God yes. I think I've got myself under control now." Madeline giggled and wrapped her arms around his neck to give him another deep, consuming kiss. His hands stroked down her hips and then with deceptive ease, he lifted her. She clung to him as he carried her to the bed in the next room. Her back hit the mattress and his weight pressed her down. "I've been dying for you to touch me since the first moment I set eyes on you." He turned onto his back. "I'm yours."

Madeline sat up. He seemed to fill her bed, his strong arms flung wide, his legs splayed. His skin was dusky against the white bed linen, his auburn hair dark. She ran her hand over his chest and down his belly. "Anywhere?"

"Everywhere." He reached up and fondled her breast until she arched her back.

"Hmm." She moved to straddle him, settling her hips atop his. Douglas's eyes rolled back in his head, but his fingers kept teasing her breast. Madeline rocked her hips, and he said something so vulgar, she laughed. "Such language," she whispered, lowering herself until her breasts were against his belly and his erection surged against her ribs. She licked across his chest, and bit down on his nipple.

"God Almighty." His arms bulged as he gripped the sheets.

"You like that?" She bit him again, this time on the tender skin at the side of his rib cage.

"Yes." His voice was strained.

She laughed softly and bent her head, tasting his skin. He kept talking, though Madeline didn't pay attention to the words; it was his tone, urgent and rough, that sent heat pulsing through her body. Now it seemed amazing that she'd withstood him so long. Now she couldn't think of anything except having him in her bed for the rest of her life.

He almost jackknifed off the bed when she ran her finger over the head of his cock, once again hard and ready. "Enough—I want to see you." His voice shook, and he reached for her. He angled his hips until his erection nudged at her. "Ride me," he ordered. "Hard."

She pushed herself up until she hovered over him on her hands and knees. "So commanding."

Sweat glistened on his face and his grin was a grimace of clenched teeth. "*Please*, darling."

She felt a moment of uncertainty. She hadn't made love to a man in over two years, and never this way. But Douglas's feverish gaze bored into her. She wrapped her hand around his cock and guided it between her legs.

His stomach spasmed. He tossed his head to one side. Madeline adjusted her knees, sinking lower, feeling him surge hard and deep inside her. "Oh," she said in a thin voice. "Oh my—"

"Ride," he growled, bucking his hips. "Put your hands on my knees." She obeyed, feeling sensual and wild as she leaned back, still moving up and down.

He raised his head. His hands ran up her thighs and then his fingers spread open her lower lips. "You own me, Mad," he rasped. His hips were still moving under her. His thumb stroked over her where their bodies joined. She quivered and almost pulled away, but he gripped her waist and steadied her, keeping her moving. "Keep on, just like that . . . I want to make you scream . . ."

"Douglas," she gasped. Her heart raced and her legs shook. She wasn't sure she could take this, her body thoroughly invaded, her every sensation swamped with the sight and sound and feel of him.

"Always, love." He sounded as strangled as she felt but his hands and hips were relentless.

"Oh—" Her thought and her speech died at the same time, as climax broke over her. Just as her ripples of pleasure began to fade, he swore ferociously and arched his back, and she felt him pulse within her. It wrung a last contraction from her body, and then another when he seized her and rolled over, pinning her beneath him.

"I knew you'd be the death of me." He kissed her, his tongue ruthlessly invading her mouth. He moved, sliding out of her and then thrusting home again. "I didn't know it would be that fiery."

"So you've expired?" She could barely speak, her breath was so ragged.

Douglas laughed and rested his forehead against hers. "Never fear, love. I shall rise again." He shifted his weight until he lay with his chest against her side. His arms went around her and pulled her tightly to him.

She pressed her lips to his chest. "I always wanted you."

"I knew it," he said under his breath, laughing when she poked him. "Thank God you succumbed to it at last."

Madeline smiled. "Would you really have gone away and stayed away, if I hadn't stopped you tonight?"

"Yes," he replied at once. "Miserably, reluctantly, and bitterly blaming myself for being the biggest fool in the world. But I would have honored your wishes."

She drew circles on his chest with her fingertip. Arthur had been strong but not nearly this sculpted. Douglas was gloriously built, all firm muscles and golden skin. His body tightened at her touch, and something inside her knotted with desire—incredibly, given that she'd already climaxed twice. "And now you've won the first wager, haven't you?"

He went very still and didn't say a word.

"I know it was a wager that brought you to my side in the first place," she went on. "Did you win a great sum?"

"Let's not talk about it," he muttered.

She raised her head and looked at him. "Are you blushing?"

"No," he said indignantly. Now his neck was red, too.

"You are." She stroked her knuckles over his flushed skin. "It won't shock me. You weren't the first to make such a wager. Do you think I don't hear the gossip?"

Something flashed in his eyes. He pushed himself up on one elbow and loomed over her, his hair falling forward to hide his expression. "It was an idiot's idle boast—"

"You're not a fool," she whispered. "You're the first to win."

"I want to be the only one to win." He brushed her hair from her face. "No—I don't want to win at all. You're not a fortress to be conquered or a game to be beaten. I deserve to lose because it was a damned stupid, rude thing to do in the first place, and if I could take it all back, I would."

*The only one to win.* Her heart gave an unsteady thump. "But you cannot. What did you win?"

"Nothing." He bent his head and kissed the base of her throat where her pulse had barely slowed.

"Don't you trust me enough to tell me?" Even as she spoke her arm stole around his neck. "Does it have something to do with our wager, about my writing?"

The look on his face was stark horror. It gave her a moment of pause. "Your reaction when I named my stake was remarkable," she went on, with some trepidation. "How did you guess?"

Douglas closed his eyes. "Please don't make me tell you."

Oh God. All her happiness and contentment drained away. Her mouth went dry. "Tell me. If you mean to stay here longer than tonight, there cannot be secrets between us."

He turned onto his back and stared at the ceiling, which did nothing for her nerves. "Remember that I'm an acknowledged idiot," he said at last.

"Very well," she murmured.

"It would also help if you forgave me right now," he added. She raised her brows in alarm, but he nodded. "Just to set the proper mood. It will give me courage."

"Then I forgive you."

Douglas took a deep breath and blew it out. "Someone placed a bounty on the identity of the author of *50 Ways to Sin*."

Madeline blinked. She stared at him, and then she laughed. It was a small giggle at first, but quickly burst into a full peal of laughter. "Lady Constance? You think I'm *Constance*?"

His expression was priceless: a mixture of discomfort, alarm, and curiosity. "Aren't you?"

It took her a moment to catch her breath, she was laughing so hard. "No," she gasped, wiping her eyes. "Although I wish I'd thought of that conceit!"

"You're truly not?"

"Truly not. What made you think I was?"

His face assumed an expression of intense relief. "You bought all that paper . . . and you wagered ownership of your writing . . ."

"Yes, I wanted you to agree!" She smiled. "Agree, and then lose."

He looked a bit piqued, but didn't respond to that. "Er . . . Your maid's name seems a great coincidence . . ." He glanced sideways at her. "Could she be . . . ?"

Madeline rolled her eyes. "If so, she is writing complete fiction. She would also be an idiot to use her own name. What else?"

He frowned. "The way you attend every *ton* party just to watch, as if you were sizing up gentlemen for discreet liaisons . . ."

"But I turn down every man who speaks to me."

"Except me." He kissed her thoroughly, as if to make her forget all that he had just said.

Madeline kissed him back, feeling much lighter. She knew about *50 Ways to Sin*. Whoever wrote it must be very daring indeed. She supposed it was plausible that someone thought she could be the author, but the effort necessary to sustain such privacy would be incredible. At the very least, servants would talk. Still, she knew it sold almost as fast as the printer could print the issues, and for that alone she envied Constance. It must be making her a fortune. "Here I thought every man in London harbored hopes of bringing the mysterious Constance to bed! What disappointment you must feel!"

Douglas shook his head. "I will never be disappointed to find myself next to you in bed."

That ended her laughter. She cupped one hand around his jaw. "Nor I, with you."

"Keep that thought in mind. Someone . . . some damned bloody guttersnipe . . . taunted me into trying to locate proof that you're Constance."

"Oh my." She laughed again. "It will be very difficult to win that wager, since there is no proof."

"I didn't wager that you *were* Constance," he quickly replied. "I only agreed that he and I would split the bounty if I found proof that you were."

Madeline smiled. She couldn't seem to stop. It all seemed so silly. "Then I forgive you, completely."

"I only wagered, just the once, that I would dance with you." Douglas seemed in the full flow of confession. "It was before I knew you at all. I still want to dance with you but I don't care a damn about the wager, and I don't intend to mention it ever again."

"Don't you like to win?"

Some of his cocksure grin returned. "I have won. You've not drawn a pistol on me or thrown me out into the street."

"Yet," she said, but with a smile that ruined it.

"Then . . ." He frowned curiously. "What writing did you plan to confess to?"

"It seems so tame now. I write the gossip for the *Intelligencer*." Douglas's expression was completely blank. "It's a small newspaper owned by a friend of my late husband's. Arthur was an investor and I inherited his shares. The newspaper was struggling and I needed some occupation. It's a great secret; I attend parties and balls in order to gather material, and I would be cut by all society if it were known."

Slowly a smile crept over his face. "Gossip. That's what you write. Good God, what a joke."

"Whoever made that wager deserves to lose," she said.

"Agreed."

A scratching at the door interrupted. Madeline gasped.

"Mr. Nash!" She scrambled out of bed and threw on her dressing gown as she hurried to the door.

Douglas sat up. "Mr. Nash?"

"Yes, my usual bed partner." She opened the door and scooped up the cat when he prowled into the room. "Isn't he a handsome fellow?"

Douglas stared at the cat, then fell back into the pillow, laughing.

"Mr. Nash," came Constance's furious whisper from the dark corridor. "Where are you, silly cat?"

"He's here." Madeline pushed open the door.

"Oh." The maid stopped short. "Quite a racket he made downstairs, wanting in. I tried to catch him before he woke you ..." Constance glanced over Madeline's shoulder and gave a tiny coy smile. "But I see he didn't. Poor George; he'll be without a position now, won't he?"

Madeline put down Mr. Nash, who was struggling. "Good night, Constance."

Her maid went back toward the stairs, shaking her head and murmuring about poor Mr. Steele, too. Madeline closed the door and regarded the scene with a tinge of amazed satisfaction. Douglas had pushed himself up on one elbow and looked virile and gorgeous in her bed. Mr. Nash lay on her pillow, regally allowing Douglas to scratch his head.

Douglas glanced up. "Mr. Nash, eh? And George and Mr. Steele? Quite a lot of fellows in this house."

"Constance has a healthy imagination. George is the footman she hoped I would hire, and Mr. Steele the butler. Neither is a real person." She slid back into bed. "I'm not the wicked widow people seem to think I am."

"Don't be hasty." He plopped the cat on the foot of the bed and pulled her close. "There's much to be said for wickedness at the right time and place."

"In bed with you?"

"Absolutely," he growled.

"I'm sorry to cost you another wager, even if a ridiculous one. If only there were some way to turn the tables on the fool who enticed you to it."

"Well," he began tentatively. "I agree—mostly because I don't want him to spread it about that you *are* Lady Constance. I did have one idea . . ."

Madeline was quiet for a minute. "Is it likely to work?"

"I think it might." He hesitated. "With your help, it might be guaranteed." And he told her his plan.

## CHAPTER SIXTEEN

The next evening, Douglas arrived with unusual punctuality at the Cartwright ball. He took a glass of wine for courage and stationed himself where he could see the whole room, and waited. Philip Albright wandered in some time later. Douglas resisted the urge to check his watch. Madeline would be here. The only question was, would Spence?

But it wasn't long before the familiar figure strolled in, his customary smirk in place. Douglas took a deep breath and made his way across the room.

"Ah, Bennet. How goes your detection?" Spence asked idly when Douglas reached him.

His gaze swept around the room. He had to wait until Madeline arrived. "So much for a polite greeting, eh?"

The other man's lip curled. "Such nice manners! I didn't expect it of you. Very well: good evening. I trust you are well?"

A flash of green at the far end of the room caught his eye. Douglas's heart jolted into his throat as Madeline stepped around a pillar with a swish of her emerald skirts. Her golden hair gleamed in the candlelight. She raised a glass of champagne to her lips, taking a leisurely glance at the guests. And when her gaze connected with his, she smiled.

Elation surged within him. Helplessly he returned her smile. He was about to take the biggest gamble of his life, but it would be worth it.

*Please God, let it be worth it, and not the biggest mistake of my life.*

"I'm very well," he said to Spence.

"Very well?" The scoundrel raised his brows. "That rings of certainty."

"It should." God, she was beautiful. Douglas watched her a moment longer before wrenching his gaze away. "I owe you some thanks for setting me on this matter."

Spence sniffed. "Make it worthwhile for both of us. That's all the thanks I want."

"Right." Douglas found Albright, standing near the musicians, and gave him a nod. "The problem is, I don't see what you've put into it besides telling me about Chesterton's bounty."

Spence turned his head sharply. "And that's worth a great deal since you would have had no idea otherwise. Nor any idea which woman to investigate."

"Well." Douglas shrugged. "That's not worth enough to compensate for the three weeks of my time. Sorry, old man; all's fair, you know."

"Bennet!" Spence seized his arm as Douglas started to walk away. "I'll bury you if you cheat me on this."

"Oh? With what shovel?" He shook off Spence's hand.

Near the center of the room Albright had sidled close to Lord Chesterton. Keeping his steps slow and unhurried, Douglas headed toward them.

"Thief," snarled Spence, following close at his heels. "Cheat!"

"I took nothing that was yours. Not one man in this room would convict me of cheating—especially not when they consider the effort I exerted."

"By God I will not allow this," the man muttered before brushing past him.

Douglas waited until Spence had almost reached Lord Chesterton before he cleared his throat. Albright had already fixed it with the musicians to delay the next dance, so few couples were assembling; Douglas stood almost alone in the center of the floor. "Ladies and gentleman," he said in a carrying voice. "A moment of your time, if you please."

Everyone seemed to turn toward him at once. His blood pounded with the thrill of the moment. He caught a fleeting glance of Madeline's expression before he forced himself to look away. "I apologize for interrupting," he went on, giving one wide-eyed matron a rueful wink and his most charming smile. "I shan't take up much of your evening. I merely feel compelled to share some news which will, I believe, amaze more than one person in this room—"

"But not as much as my announcement!" Spencer's angry shout cut him off.

Douglas obediently fell quiet and tried to look shocked as his onetime friend strode up to him, eyes flashing. *Go on*, Douglas silently dared him. *Do it.*

Spence glared at him before spinning on his heel toward Lord Chesterton. "My lord, I believe you offered a bounty."

Spence hadn't spoken very loudly but in the expectant hush of the ballroom every word carried. Chesterton's face went dead white, like a man suddenly regretting a long-ago outburst. "This is not the place . . ."

With another furious look at Douglas, Spence held up one hand. "Does that mean you don't intend to honor it?"

The intake of breath around the room was audible.

Chesterton's lips barely moved as he replied. "I always honor my word, sir."

Good Lord, it was better than he'd hoped. Spence was so angry he was defying any sort of propriety or discretion to beat Douglas to the point. This would be branded on his name for years to come.

"Spence," Douglas began.

The man threw up his hand. "I've discovered the name you seek, my lord," he said rapidly. "Shall we retire to a more private location to discuss the matter?"

"You have not!" Albright scoffed, making Lord Chesterton start. "Anyone can produce a name; he could make one up on the spot."

"The evidence is in my favor," Spence retorted.

"What evidence?"

Spence's eyes darted back to Douglas. "That is for his lordship to hear."

Chesterton was as still as a statue. "I have no idea what you mean, sir . . ."

For the first time Spence looked around at the breathlessly

watching guests. Every pair of eyes in the room was fixed on him. Even people who had no idea what bounty he was talking about were eager to know the answer—and Douglas was quite sure they would discover every lurid thing about Chesterton's offer before the end of the evening, after this little drama. "Perhaps we should speak privately—"

"So he won't have to defend his 'evidence,'" said Albright sotto voce.

William Spence drew himself up, squaring his shoulders. "Mrs. Madeline Wilde."

People gasped. Douglas allowed himself a quick glance in her direction; the crowd was already easing away from her, giving him a clear view. She stood staring, her beautiful lips parted and her eyes blank with apparent shock. It physically hurt him to see her suffer this public denouncement, even though she had agreed to this part of the plan.

"How dare you," he growled at Spence, not having to feign his anger.

Spence barked with laughter. "How dare I? When you came tonight to tell Lord Chesterton the very same thing— that *she* is the woman who defamed him!"

Douglas took a step back. "I most certainly did not. Tonight I came . . ." He turned toward Madeline. She was still there, rooted to the spot, with one hand now at her breast, looking as if she'd been betrayed. "Tonight I had a very different sort of declaration in mind."

"You said—" Spence's face went slack as he realized.

"I know I've got a bit of a reputation." Never taking his eyes from her face, Douglas started toward Madeline. "I won't say I didn't earn it, but what I did to earn it is all in the past. And it shall stay in the past because I've gone and lost my heart."

A blush raced up her face as he came to a halt in front of her. The people around her, who had withdrawn a few steps when Spence cried out her name, were goggling at him with every sort of expression from disapproval to shocked delight.

"You astonish everyone," Madeline said in a low voice. "Public announcements of attachment!"

Slowly he grinned. He hadn't told her all of his plan; she was expecting a gallant defense of her name. But the moment she agreed to his mad plan, put her trust in him and made love to him and slept in his arms, he knew. She was no ordinary woman. For the first time in his life, he couldn't imagine life without a woman in his house, in his bed, in his arms—*this* woman. Still, he didn't know what her answer would be, and his heart kicked against his ribs in nervous hope. "It's even more than that. It's a proposal of marriage."

A lady in the crowd let out a little shriek. A matron standing nearby put her hand on her bosom and smiled.

Madeline's eyes went wide in shock. "That is a very large risk."

"With a very large reward, if my luck holds." He went down on one knee and held his hand out, palm up. He hoped she didn't notice it shook slightly. "Will you consider it, my love?"

"No," she said softly. Thankfully she went on before his heart had a chance to stop. "I would like to accept." And she took his hand.

He rose and pressed his lips to her wrist as a murmur rippled through the crowd. "I love you," he whispered. "Desperately."

Her eyes glowed with sparks of gold. "You'd better. We'll never be spoken of again without some mention of this evening."

"I have no objection to that."

"I thought you weren't a marrying sort of man," she murmured unsteadily.

"Until I met you, I wasn't. Now . . ." He rubbed his thumb over her third finger, where his ring would soon be. "Now I look forward to it."

A hand on his shoulder jerked him around. Spence looked angry enough to kill him. "You lied to me."

"Mr. Spence." A tall and rather imposing servant glided up to them. "Lord Chesterton would like a word—privately."

Spence's furious gaze veered to Madeline and then back to Douglas. "Very well."

"And with you, Mr. Bennet," added the footman.

"Of course." He offered Madeline his arm. "Shall you come along, or do you want to miss the fireworks?"

"I wouldn't miss this for the world," she breathed, twining her arm through his.

They followed Spence. The hiss of whispers in their wake was deafening. Lord Chesterton was waiting in a small parlor, his face set in stern lines, and Philip Albright leaned against the mantel with the air of a man about to enjoy a good show. "Explain yourself," spat Chesterton as soon as the door was closed. "How *dare* you mention that bounty in the presence of so many ladies?"

Spence had obviously made an effort to control himself

and organize a defense. "I was deceived," he said stiffly. "By Bennet and, I suspect, by Albright. I apologize, my lord."

"You must be the greatest idiot in London. What deception did they practice on you that you felt at liberty to bring my name into your scandalous behavior?"

Spence shot another venomous look at Douglas. "It doesn't signify, my lord."

"No," retorted Lord Chesterton in disdain. "You merely stood up and accused the Duke of Canton's goddaughter of being that vile liar Lady Constance."

Everyone turned to look at her, Douglas in some surprise. The Duke of Canton's goddaughter? He'd heard the rumors about her mother and Canton, but not that. Madeline merely looked quietly outraged.

"I told you she wasn't, Spence," Albright said. "Never saw any proof of it."

"Were you searching?" Chesterton looked astounded.

Albright nodded. "Spence went 'round saying she must be Lady Constance, and offering to split your bounty with anyone who could prove it."

The older man flushed and turned on Douglas. "And you, sir? I presume you were involved in this as well."

"Spence made me the same offer." He glanced at Madeline. "Happily, I lost interest in that endeavor and found something far more dear."

"So I see." Chesterton was also watching her. "I apologize for the scene you just endured, madam. I deeply regret any part I may have played in causing it."

She curtsied. "You are very kind, but I bear no ill will toward you, my lord."

He inclined his head in gracious acknowledgment before turning back to Spence. "You, however . . ."

"I was deceived," said Spence again. "Mr. Bennet may stand here now acting the part of a lovesick fool, but for a fortnight he has repeatedly assured me he was in possession of more and more evidence that Mrs. Wilde is Lady Constance. I would never have presumed to act as I did—"

"If you hadn't been afraid he was about to cut you out of your share?" Chesterton's tone was frosty. "Perhaps you wish to ask the lady directly." He waved one hand as Spence froze. "Go on, man. You had no compunction naming her in public."

Slowly Spence faced Madeline. Douglas felt her fingers grip his arm, but her expression remained composed. "Are you the infamous Lady Constance, author of *50 Ways to Sin*?"

Her gaze was cool, disdainful, and insulted. "I promise you, I am not."

Spence gave a jerky bow. "I humbly apologize for my mistake, madam."

"Get out," said Chesterton in a soft, deadly voice.

Moving as if his limbs were made of wood, Spence went. As he opened the door, Albright called after him, "I'll come 'round tomorrow to collect on our wager, shall I?" Spence paused a moment in the doorway, then continued on his way without a word. Beaming with satisfaction, Albright bid them all farewell and left.

"I trust," said Lord Chesterton, "this will be the end of the matter."

Douglas privately thought it would live on for months in drawing rooms across London. "I hope so as well."

"It is over for me," Madeline concurred. "Although, I must

say . . . if Lady Constance truly did model her characters on actual persons, she couldn't have chosen a finer one than you, my lord."

Interest sparked in Chesterton's eyes. "Oh?" Then he glanced at Douglas, and a faint smile crossed his face. "Ah well; too late for that." He bowed. "Good evening, Mrs. Wilde. Mr. Bennet."

He left them alone, closing the door behind him. Douglas let out his breath and grinned. "You're as brilliant as you are beautiful, love."

She laughed. "Am I? I certainly wouldn't have believed any charge that I was writing *50 Ways to Sin*."

"I was very torn," he said somberly. "On one hand, if you were, Spence would win, and I wanted to prevent that at all costs." He made a face. "However, if you were, it would also demonstrate a naughty imagination and a certain . . . uninhibited generosity I find utterly bewitching—"

"I never said I *couldn't* write something like that," she murmured.

"Unfortunately that would ruin the new respectability we shall have to cultivate if we're ever to outlive tonight's gossip." He drew her toward him. "But I would never dream of impeding your creative wishes. If your muse leads you to write wicked, naughty fantasies about me, I would never argue. In fact, I would read them over and over."

"Oh?" She braced her hands on his chest. "You would prefer to read than do?"

"No." He dragged her against him in spite of her hands— not that she put much effort into her resistance. "We can do both. Every author needs a muse, after all . . ."

"I don't think much about writing when you do that," she said on a sigh, letting him kiss his way down her neck. Her hands had gone from holding him away to clinging.

"What *do* you think about?" he murmured with interest.

"It's hard to think at all." She waited until he raised his head. "But mostly . . . I think of how much I love you."

He was the luckiest bloke in Britain. "That's all I want."

Don't miss the other romances
in Caroline Linden's deliciously sexy
Scandals series:

## *Love and Other Scandals*

Tristan, Lord Burke, has no intention of ever marrying, especially not a droll, sharp-witted spinster like Joan Bennet. If only their clashes didn't lead to kissing . . . and embraces . . . and a passion neither can resist.

## *It Takes a Scandal*

Mysterious and reclusive, Sebastian Vane is rumored to be a thief and a murderer—not the sort of man an heiress like Abigail Weston would marry. But even the fiercest scandal is no match for love . . .

## Love in the Time of Scandal
### Coming Soon!

Penelope Weston has her heart set on finding passion and adventure along with true love. Benedict Lennox, Lord Atherton, wants just the opposite, no matter how tempting he finds Penelope. But Fate seems to be throwing them together, until scandal leads to marriage—and that could lead to so much more than either of them ever imagined.

Want more *scandalous* romance?

Keep reading for a sneak peek at
*USA Today* best-selling and RITA® Award–winning author
Caroline Linden's next novel,

*Love in the Time of Scandal*

Coming June 2015
from Avon Romance

Some people were born with an acute appreciation of the little things in life: a good book, a beautiful garden, a quiet peaceful home. Nothing pleased them more than improving their minds through reading, or practicing an art such as painting or playing an instrument, or helping the sick and infirm. Such people were truly noble and inspiring.

Penelope Weston was not one of those people.

In fact, she felt very much the opposite of noble or inspiring as she stood at the side of Lady Hunsford's ballroom and glumly watched the beautiful couples whirling around the floor. She wasn't envious . . . much . . . but she was decidedly bored. This was a new feeling for her. Once balls and parties had been the most exciting thing in the world. She had thrilled at sharing the latest gossip and discussing the season's fashions with her older sister, Abigail, and their friend Joan Bennet. None of the three of them had been popular young ladies, so they always had plenty of time to talk at balls, interrupted only occasionally by a gentleman asking one of them to dance.

At the time, they had all openly wished for more gentlemen to ask them to dance, and to call on them, flowers in hand, and beg for their company on a drive in the park. No one wanted to be a spinster all her life, after all. Whenever Joan fell into despair over her height, or Abigail fretted that only fortune hunters would want her, Penelope loyally maintained that there existed a man who would find Joan's tall, statuesque figure appealing, and a man who would want Abigail for more than her dowry.

Well, now she'd been proven right. Joan had married the very rakish Viscount Burke, and Abigail was absolutely moonstruck in love with her new husband, Sebastian. Penelope was very happy for both of them, she really was . . . but she was also feeling left out for the first time in her life. Her sister was only a year older than she, and they had been the best of friends her entire life—and now Abigail was happily rusticating in Richmond, cultivating the quieter society that made Penelope want to run screaming from the room. Joan's bridegroom had swept her off on a very exciting and exotic wedding trip to Italy, which Penelope envied fiercely but obviously could not share. And that left her alone, standing at the side of ballrooms once more, but this time without her dearest friends to pass the time.

"Miss Weston! Oh, Miss Weston, what a pleasure to see you tonight!"

Penelope roused herself from her brooding thoughts and smiled. Frances Lockwood beamed back, cheeks pink from dancing. Frances was on the brink of her first season, still starry-eyed at the social whirl of London. "And you, Miss Lockwood. I hope you are well."

The younger girl nodded. "Very well! I think this is the most beautiful ballroom I've ever seen!"

Penelope kept smiling. Just three years ago she'd been every bit as wide-eyed and delighted as Miss Lockwood. It was both amusing and disconcerting to see how she must have looked to everyone back then. "It is a very fine room. Lady Hunsford has quite an eye for floral arrangements."

"Indeed!" Miss Lockwood agreed eagerly. "And the musicians are very talented."

"They are." Penelope felt much older than her twenty-one years, discussing flower arrangements and musicians. Her mother was probably making the very same comments to her friends.

Miss Lockwood sidled a step closer. "And the gentlemen are so very handsome, don't you think?"

Now Penelope's smile grew a bit rigid. Frances Lockwood was the granddaughter of a viscount. Her father was a mere gentleman, and her mother was a banker's daughter, but that noble connection made all the difference. Penelope's father had been an attorney before he made his fortune investing in coal canals, and the grime of that origin had never fully washed away. The Lockwoods were received everywhere; Frances, with her dowry less than half the size of Penelope's, was considered a very eligible heiress. Not that Penelope wanted Frances's suitors—who were silly young men with empty pockets, for the most part—but it set something inside her roiling when she saw the way they fawned over her friend.

"There are many handsome gentlemen in London," Penelope said aloud. There were, although none near this part of the ballroom, where the unmarried ladies congregated. If Joan were here, they could discuss the scandalous rakes lounging elegantly at the far end of the room, closer to the wine. But Frances was only seventeen and would fall into a blushing stammer if Penelope openly admired the way Lord Fenton's trousers fit his thighs.

Frances nodded, a beatific smile on her face. She edged a little closer to Penelope's side and dropped her voice. "Miss Weston . . . may I confide in you? You've been very kind to me, and I do so look up to you for advice—well, you know, on how to deal with gentlemen who are only interested in One Thing."

Oh dear. Frances meant the fortune hunters who clustered around her. Penelope tried not to heave a sigh. Unfortunately she had too much experience of those men, and too little experience of real suitors. She was probably the least suited person to be giving advice, but Frances persisted in asking her. "Is another one bothering you? If so, you must send him on his way at once. Such a man will never make you happy if all he cares for is your fortune or your connections."

"Oh no, I know that very well," replied Frances earnestly. "I've turned away Mr. Whittington and Sir Thomas Philpot and even Lord Dartmond, although my mama was not very pleased by the last one. Only when I explained to her that you had turned him down as the very lowest of fortune hunters did she relent."

The Earl of Dartmond was at least forty, with a pernicious gambling habit. Mrs. Lockwood was a fool if she even considered him for her daughter, earl or not. "I'm sure you'll be very happy you did, when you meet a kinder gentleman who cares for you."

The younger girl nodded, her face brightening again. "I

know! I know, because I have met him! Oh, Miss Weston, he's the handsomest man you ever saw. Always so smartly attired, and the very best horseman I've ever seen, and a music lover—he listened to me play for almost an hour the last time he called, and said I was a marvel on the pianoforte." Frances looked quite rapturous; she was very fond of the pianoforte and practiced for an hour each day, something Penelope couldn't fathom surviving, let alone enjoying. "And what's more, he's heir to an earl and has no need of my fortune. Mama is so pleased, and Papa, too. He's been calling on me for at least a fortnight now, always with a small gift or posy, and he's the most charming, delightful gentleman I could imagine!"

Penelope nodded, hoping it was all true. "How wonderful. I told you there were true gentlemen out there. They just require some hunting."

Frances laughed almost giddily. "There are! My other friends were so very scandalized when I refused to receive Mr. Whittington, because he's the most graceful dancer even if he is horribly in debt, but you were entirely correct. I credit your wise advice for the happiness I now feel—indeed, for the very great match I'm about to make! May I present you to him? He's to attend tonight."

For a moment Penelope felt like saying no. It was bad enough that she had to feel old and unwanted next to Frances. Her friend was sweet and kind, but also somewhat silly and naïve. It was bad enough to see Joan and Abigail marry deliciously handsome men; Penelope loved them and wanted them to be happy. She also wanted Frances to be happy, but tonight it just felt a bit hard to see Frances find her ideal man and be swept off her feet in her very first year in London, while Penelope had been overlooked for three years now by all but the most calculating fortune hunters.

But that was petty. She mustered another smile. "Of course. You know I always like to meet handsome men." Frances's eyes widened at the last, and Penelope hastily added, "I'm especially pleased to meet one who adores you."

Frances's smile returned. "He does, Miss Weston, I really believe he does! He's even hinted that he means to speak to my papa soon." A very pretty blush colored her cheeks. "How should I respond, if he asks me about that?"

"If you want to marry him, you should tell your father that he's the man for you. And stand by your conviction," she added. "Parents may not always understand your heart, so you must be sure to tell them emphatically."

"Yes, of course." Frances nodded. "I hope you approve of him, Miss Weston."

"Your approval is what matters." Penelope wondered if she had ever been so anxious for someone else's validation of her opinion. She would have to ask Abigail, the next time she saw her sister.

"I see him," said Frances with a little cry of nervous delight. "Oh my, he's *so* handsome! And his uniform is very dashing! Don't you think so?"

Penelope followed her companion's gaze and saw a group of the King's Life Guards, making their entrance with some swagger. Instinctively her mouth flattened. She'd met a few of them last summer, when one of their number, Benedict Lennox, Lord Atherton, had courted her sister. Penelope was sure he'd never been in love with Abigail, and when Abigail confessed her love for another man, Lord Atherton reacted like a thwarted child. Penelope hoped he wasn't in the crowd, but then she caught sight of his dark head.

She repressed the urge to walk the other way. She hadn't seen him since they last parted, when he'd reluctantly helped solve a years-old mystery that had tarred the name of the man Abigail loved. Sebastian Vane had stood accused of stealing a large sum of money from Lord Atherton's father, and Atherton himself had done nothing to disprove it—even though he'd once been Sebastian's dearest friend. Penelope grudgingly admitted that Atherton had been fairly decent after that, but she still thought he was insincere and always had an eye out for his own interest, whatever truth or justice demanded.

It wasn't until Atherton turned and looked toward them that Penelope realized she was staring at him. She quickly averted her gaze and turned her body slightly, hoping he hadn't actually noticed her. However, that only gave her a good view of Frances's face, which was glowing with joy.

Because . . . Penelope closed her eyes, praying she was wrong. Because her brain was fitting together details, just moments too late, and they were adding up to one dreadful conclusion. Atherton was heir to the Earl of Stratford, who was a very wealthy man. He was appallingly handsome, which Penelope only acknowledged with deep disgust. And when she stole a quick glance under her eyelashes, she saw that he was heading directly for the pair of them.

Oh Lord. What could she say now?

"Miss Lockwood." Penelope gritted her teeth as he bowed. His voice was smooth and rich, the sort of voice a woman wanted to hear whispering naughty things in her ear. "How delightful to see you this evening."

"I am the one delighted, my lord." Blushing and beaming, Frances dipped a curtsy. "May I present to you my good friend, Miss Penelope Weston?"

His gaze moved to her without a flicker of surprise. He'd seen her, and was obviously more prepared for the meeting than she was. "Of course. But Miss Weston and I are already acquainted."

Penelope curtsied as Frances gaped. "Indeed, my lord."

"I—I didn't know that," stammered Frances, looking anxious again. "Are you very good friends? Oh dear, I wish I had known!"

"No, we hardly know each other," said Penelope before he could answer. "It was a passing acquaintance, really."

Atherton's brilliant blue eyes lingered on her a moment before returning to Frances. "The Westons own property near Stratford Court."

"Then you're merely neighbors?" asked Frances hopefully. "In Richmond?"

"A river divides us," Penelope assured her. "A very wide river."

Atherton glanced at her sharply, but thankfully didn't argue. "Yes, in Richmond. Unfortunately I'm kept here in London most of the year. I believe my sister Samantha is better acquainted with Miss Weston."

"Indeed," said Penelope with a pointed smile. "I hope Lady Samantha is well."

"Yes," said Lord Atherton after a moment's pause. "She is."

Too late Penelope remembered about Samantha. In

their zeal to clear Sebastian Vane's name so Abigail could marry him, the Weston girls had inadvertently resurrected a dark secret of Samantha's, one her brother had claimed would lead to dire consequences for her. Penelope hadn't wanted to cause trouble for Samantha, but Sebastian had been accused of murder and thievery; Abigail's happiness depended on exonerating him, and Samantha was the only person who could help. Penelope cringed to have brought it up, but Atherton did say she was well, so the consequences must not have been as bad as he'd predicted. Still, she did truly like Samantha—far more than the lady's brother— and she was sorry to have been so cavalier with her name.

For a tense moment they seemed frozen there, Penelope biting her tongue, Frances looking troubled, and Atherton staring at her with a strange intensity. He shook it off first. "Miss Lockwood, I hope you've saved me a dance."

Frances's smile returned, although a little less brilliantly than before. "Of course, my lord. I am free the next two."

"Excellent." He gazed warmly at her, and Frances seemed to sway on her feet.

Penelope had to work hard to keep from rolling her eyes. How could she escape this? Thankfully she caught sight of a familiar face across the room, causing her to smile widely in relief. "You must excuse me, I see a dear friend just arriving. Miss Lockwood, Lord Atherton." She bobbed a quick farewell and all but ran across the room.

Olivia Townsend was one of Penelope's favorite people in the world. She was only a few years older than Abigail, and had been like an older sister to the two Weston girls for as long as Penelope could remember. Olivia's family had lived near the Westons and all four children had been fast friends. But while Penelope's family had prospered—greatly—since then, Olivia's had not. At a fairly young age, she'd made a hasty marriage of dubious happiness to a charming but feckless fellow, Henry Townsend, who managed to run through his modest fortune with shocking speed before his death a few years ago. Since then, Olivia had lived very modestly. It was a surprise to see her here tonight, in fact, as she didn't often attend balls.

"Olivia!"

Her friend was scanning the room and didn't seem to have noticed her approach; she jumped at Penelope's exclamation. "Oh," she said in a constricted voice. "You startled me."

She blinked. "I can see that. Whom were you expecting, an ogre?"

For a moment Olivia's face froze, as if she had in fact been on guard, but then she smiled ruefully. With a shake of her head, she turned her back to the room and squeezed Penelope's hand. "Forgive me; I was woolgathering. Are you enjoying the ball?"

"Well enough." Penelope peered closely at her. "What's wrong? You looked worried."

Olivia waved one hand. "It was nothing. How kind of you to leave your friends and join me."

Penelope barely kept back her snort. "I don't know how I could have stayed. You'll never guess who Miss Lockwood's new suitor is."

"Who?"

"Lord Atherton," whispered Penelope, after a cautious glance backward. She'd already let her temper get the better of her once tonight, and wouldn't put it past him to overhear every slighting word she spoke about him.

Olivia looked surprised. "Atherton? The gentleman who courted—?"

"The same," said Penelope grimly. "And my sister felt so cruel to turn him down! I shall have to write to her at once and assure her that, far from suffering a malaise, he's found a younger, sillier girl to marry."

"Now, Pen, you don't know that. He may be deeply attached to her."

She couldn't stop the snort this time. "She is certainly attached to him. He's the perfect man, in her telling. I don't know how I could have held my composure if I'd known who she was talking about. He sits and listens to her practice the pianoforte—can you imagine?"

"Perhaps he enjoys it." Penelope widened her eyes in patent disbelief. "Perhaps he's so smitten with her, he would be content just to sit and gaze at her," Olivia added. "It could happen."

"Huh." Penelope made a face. Just the thought of Lord Atherton sitting and staring at her was enough to make her skin prickle.

"Well, it's Miss Lockwood's cross to bear," said Olivia practically.

"But if he marries her, I'll have to see him from time to time." Frances might be young and naïve, but she was endearing all the same, and Penelope did like her.

Olivia laughed and tucked Penelope's arm through hers. "Perhaps she'll become disenchanted and change her mind about him."

She caught sight of Lord Atherton, leading Frances about

the floor in a quadrille. Frances was fairly radiating adoration as she gazed up at him. It took Penelope some effort to quell the urge to run over and warn Frances not to fall for his very handsome smile, or athletic figure, or disgustingly perfect face. "For her sake as well as mine," she grumbled, "I hope so."

## About the Author

CAROLINE LINDEN was born a reader, not a writer. She earned a math degree from Harvard University and wrote computer software before turning to writing fiction. Twelve years, sixteen books, three Red Sox championships, and one dog later, she has never been happier with her decision. Her books have won the NEC Reader's Choice Beanpot Award, the Daphne du Maurier Award, the NJRW Golden Leaf award, and RWA's RITA® Award. Since she never won any prizes in math, she takes this as a sign that her decision was also a smart one. Visit her online at *www.CarolineLinden.com*.

Discover great authors, exclusive offers, and more at hc.com.